The Life and Chaos of a Retired Old God

Humour, Magic and Old Gods who should know better: A Collection of Ernie Smith Short Stories

Jemma Weir

Jemma Weir

Also By

HIGHLAND RIFT PACK

Buried by Earth

Bitten by Frost

Battered by Storms

ERNIE SMITH

Finding Death's Scythe

In the Cards

The Life and Chaos of a Retired Old God – Short Story
Collection

STANDALONE

Wishing For Truths – Short Story

Contents

AUTHOR'S NOTES

This book is written in British English. That means that apologize is apologise and realizes is realises. But don't panic, I've seen another author provide the solution:

Zzzzzzzzzzzzzzzzzzzzzzzzzzzzzzzzzzzzzzzz

You now have the Z's you need to replace the S's—enjoy!

Now, onto the book itself. This is a collection of stories I wrote from the point of view of Ernie Smith, an old God living in a retirement home. They were originally published individually between 2021 to 2022, with Finding Death's Scythe and In the Cards often being found for free.

I wrote the first eight stories with my grandad in mind, and each of the initial stories has an author's note about what part of his quirkiness I included in that story. These might have changed slightly from the original version, as they were initially at the end of the story rather than before.

Each of the first seven stories can be read in any order, but I would recommend reading all of them before reading Time for Change.

The bonus story, and the Flashes of Ernie, can also be read in an order. Though I will add that for the flashes, if you read Finding Death's Scythe you will get introduced to a character that appears in some of them.

I hope you enjoy Ernie and his adventures that don't quite go to plan, and if you do, don't forget to leave a review and let others know you liked it.

Finding Death's Scythe

Author's Notes

My granddad was a memorable, quirky, and somewhat awkward man. This story weaves in one of those quirks in a way I am sure he would have appreciated—a never ending, constantly changing, and always exaggerated story, in which he was usually the hero.

Rab might not resemble my grandad in any other way, but it was fun to include this aspect of him in the story.

This is for all those granddads out there who live on in our memories.

FINDING DEATH'S SCYTHE

Ernie ignored the disconcerting feeling of being watched as he turned another corner—the portraits that lined the walls were just trying to intimidate him. Except for the one who was snoring, he was asleep against his frame.

The new hallway looked like all the others, grey on grey, with more pictures, and an endless looking path in front of him. Ernie took a half-dozen steps, then turned at a right angle and walked through the gap in the wall.

Ahead, finally, he could see the exit. Even better, the way looked clear. Ernie walked slowly, ready to dash across the small stretch of open space.

'Hello?' The voice ricocheted across the paintings, echoing down the corridor, making Ernie freeze mid-step.

Ernie sighed, then turned slowly to look at the figure, then raised his eyes a little higher to find the face. He blinked—he supposed you could call it a face.

The figure cleared his throat nervously.

'Why are you so tall?' Ernie asked carefully.

Something scraped against the tiled floor, and the figure shrunk a little. That was to say, his head no longer brushed the pale grey ceiling. 'I was experimenting,' it said sullenly.

'And the Voice?' Ernie used the capital letter. It deserved it. The way it bounced around first before reaching him was impressive, if a bit ostentatious.

'It's good to try something new.' The voice was now ordinary, and the figure was almost human sized.

Ernie should have stopped there, but he just couldn't help himself. 'And the clothes?'

The figure sighed, and the black cloth shimmered into plain trousers and a white button-up shirt. His face, now fully visible, was that of a middle-aged, average-looking man. The sort that you immediately forgot as soon as you looked away. It said a lot about him that Death chose this as his regular face. He was not the only Death, of course, but this Death had been storing something Ernie needed.

'Did you come here just to insult my creativity?' Death asked, crossing his arms. The portrait behind him echoed the movement. 'Or did you want something?'

'I just stopped by for a visit,' Ernie said, putting on his best bewildered old man *if you correct me, I will bash your brains in with my walking stick* face. It worked better on humans, but even immortals could forget who they were dealing with at times.

Death's eyes lit up, mouth opening to speak, but Ernie got there first. 'But you were out, and I have to go now.'

'Ahh, unfortunate,' Death said, face dropping. 'Will you visit again soon?'

'Sure,' Ernie said, taking a step back. For them, 'soon' was a somewhat relative term. A hundred years could be soon, he supposed.

GARD VILLAGE—SENIOR LIVING WAS a large, sprawling building that had seen better days. The spring weather had encouraged someone to plant a small patch of flowers around the sign. It might eventually hide the graffitied letters of '*mid*'.

The communal living room was almost empty as Ernie entered. In one corner, a young doctor was comforting a duty nurse, her eyelashes glistening with tears. Standing between them in his boxer shorts was Fred. He was just on the far side of ninety; stringy and gnarled might have described him when he had been wearing clothes. Without them, he looked like an old tree that had been bent over by the wind.

Fred had died during the night, and his ghost self was trying to convince the doctor that he was not dead. He either hadn't noticed, or didn't care, that neither of them could see him. Ernie had expected Death to have collected the soul already. It was why he'd chosen today to borrow—

'Where is it?' Death said from behind Ernie.

Ernie froze, the feeling of déjà vu making his skin crawl as he forced his hand not to go to his pocket. There was no way Death could know it was missing already.

'I don't know what you're talking about,' Ernie said quietly, turning around. Going by the lack of reaction from the doctor, Death had not made himself visible to the humans, but Ernie was in clear view of the nurses.

'My Scythe. You stole it. I was late picking up one soul, and you want to do my job for me?' Death growled.

'Are you dead too?' Fred asked, walking through the sofa without appearing to notice.

'No, I'm Death,' Death said, the image flickering for a heartbeat.

'That's what I asked. Are you dead?' Fred frowned, scratching his ear as he stared at Death, before turning to Ernie. 'Why are you glowing?'

'I'm Death. Not dead, just Death,' Death said, eye twitching. 'I would have collected you, but someone thought it would be funny to steal my Scythe.'

'You have a Scythe?' Fred asked, raising a hairy eyebrow.

Ernie wisely said nothing as Death's face turned scarlet, his glare now aimed solidly at Fred. At least Ernie knew for sure that he hadn't stolen the Scythe.

'Very well. Do you think you can do better? Have at it. It's not an easy job being Death.' Death waved his arms wildly. Fred ducked before he got smacked in the face. 'I'm not collecting another soul until you bring my Scythe back.'

'I don't have your Scythe,' Ernie said, but Death was already gone.

The nurse coughed loudly, making Ernie sigh and glance in their direction. Both were looking at him oddly. One of the good things about being old was that you were suddenly considered quirky for actions that forty years earlier would have been strange, and occasionally even criminal.

Ernie smiled at them. After a silent glare, the nurse turned her attention back to the doctor. Ernie wasn't one of the regular troublemakers, and today the doctor was far more interesting.

'So that was the real Death then?' Fred asked, his foot sinking slightly into the bile green carpet. 'Not quite what I expected, really.'

'Rude, that's what he is,' Rab said from behind Ernie.

Ernie turned slowly, hoping he had heard wrong. He hadn't. Rab and two other deceased residents were looking about the room, frowning. They were souls that Death had already collected.

Spinning on his heel, Ernie stalked away to throw himself into an armchair in the corner. He was not getting involved. If Death had lost his Scythe, he could bloody well find it himself.

The ghosts followed him, still talking.

ERNIE TRIED TO IGNORE the ghosts. He really did. But it was hard to ignore someone diving through you because they thought you were the white light they were meant to cross through. Or Fred's incessant babbling.

'Look, I know I'm not really dead. You just have to show me where my body is, and I'll hop right in,' Fred said, so close he was half inside Ernie's shoulder, sending a bone-deep chill into him.

Very briefly, Ernie considered asking one of the other Deaths to remove the ghosts. However, he suspected his Death had already thought of that, and not only would they refuse to collect the souls, but they might leave him stuck with more. Ernie shuddered at the thought; these people had been bad enough when they'd been alive, but now they were dead, there was no way to avoid them.

Ernie turned the page on the book in his hands, subtlety shifting away from Fred, so he was no longer overlapping.

One of the ghosts leapt through Ernie again, a surge of energy knocking the book from his hands.

'Enough,' Ernie said, drawing a sullen glare from the nurse. She'd not forgiven Ernie for distracting the doctor earlier.

The ghost just stared at Ernie like he was being stupid and leapt through him again. This wasn't working. He had to get rid of the ghosts. With a sigh, he realised that meant he'd have to find who took the damned Scythe and give it back to Death.

'We're leaving,' Ernie announced to the ghosts, quieter this time so the nurse didn't decide he needed extra pills.

'Not yet, she's gonna do it any second,' Rab said, staring intently at the card table near the centre of the room, in particular Betty's hands. Her ability to cheat at poker was one of the banes of their retirement.

'You can watch it later.' Ernie sighed as one of the old men did another leap through him. The man fell to the floor in a pile. 'It's time to find Death's Scythe.'

'You don't know where it is?' Rab asked, half turning away from the card table.

'Not exactly,' Ernie said. There was a relatively limited pool of people stupid enough to steal Death's Scythe. 'But I know where to start.'

'Can we stop by my body on the way?' Fred asked.

'No, but we're going to a bar,' Ernie said. All the ghosts turned to him, perking up at the idea.

'I'm in,' Rab said, grinning to show all his missing teeth.

THE RABID RABBIT WAS a small hole-in-the-wall bar that was bigger on the inside than it looked from the street. Any human who wandered in often thought it was an incredible illusion. At least they did until they were fed enough absinthe that they passed out.

When they woke in a nearby alley where the non-human patrons had left them, so they didn't have to clean up the mess, the hallucination was more of a concern. Strangely, they didn't know how to deal with the idea that eight-feet tall ogres and foot tall pixies might actually exist.

The bouncer at the door looked Ernie up and down, blinking slowly. There was enough of a layer of otherness about Ernie that the bouncer would know he wasn't human, but not much else. The bouncer sighed and nodded, then he turned to the ghosts.

'No ghosts,' he said in a deep voice.

The ghosts took immediate offence at the bouncer's words, even though they had complained the entire way about how they'd wanted to figure out how Betty cheated at poker so well.

'They're with me,' Ernie said reluctantly.

'You're taking responsibility for anything they do?'

Ernie nodded, gritting his teeth. But really, it wasn't as if the ghosts could touch anything. How much damage could they cause?

The bouncer's lips thinned, looking Ernie up and down again, but he moved aside to let them through.

Inside was a chaotic collection of myths that had seen better days. Most nursing a glass. The ghosts stared, open-mouthed. Except for Rab, who immediately headed straight for the young woman in the corner, with a smile that showed his last few teeth.

'Where do you think you're going?' A voice shouted above the noise. The speaker was head and shoulders taller than most men and almost double the width. He leaned against the bar that ran half the length of the room, one hand on his glass.

Rab ignored the man, walking straight through him. Which only made him angrier.

'I'm looking for something that was stolen,' Ernie said, trying to pull the focus away from the ghosts as he looked around at the mismatched tables. Two heads shot up, suddenly interested in what Ernie was saying.

'Your kind is not welcome here,' the burly man said, ignoring Ernie's question as he pushed away from the bar, glaring at the ghosts.

'Our kind?' Fred said, looking at his fellow ghosts, then stepped closer, shoulder passing through Ernie as he did. 'We could wipe the floor with you.'

The man laughed. Fred's jaw tightened as he stepped closer. He hadn't been tall when he'd been alive, and compared to this man, he was a child.

With a surprising amount of agility, Fred threw a punch at the man's midsection. Unsurprisingly, he passed straight through.

Fred's arms pinwheeled as he tried to regain his balance. He stumbled to a halt in the centre of the wooden bar, right where the man's glass sat. The glass tilted, then settled back down again with a click. Fred noticed and repeated the movement again. The glass moved with him.

'Don't,' the man warned with a growl, but he didn't move.

Fred grinned, tilting his hips at an angle Ernie doubted he had managed in years. The glass fell with a clatter, splashing onto the man's jacket.

The man shouted, backing away, cursing, trying to wipe at the whisky. Unable to touch Fred, he focused instead on Ernie.

'No one brings ghosts here,' the man said, snarling as he took a swing.

Ernie sighed, catching the punch in his fist, then kicked the burly man backwards. The bar splintered as the burly man crashed into it. The smell of beer filled the air as a tap split, spraying brown liquid and foam over everything. The bartender cursed, jumping clear, glaring at Ernie.

The patrons looked between Ernie and the burly man. Ernie might have looked like an eighty-year-old man, but it was really just an illusion. The entire bar had just re-evaluated him. A tingle of excitement filled the room at the prospect of a fight.

There was a moment of collective breath-holding as they exchanged glances. The hiss of spraying beer filled the silence. That might have been the end of it. Years later, as Ernie looked back, he would remember that 'almost' with great clarity.

It started with a cheer. Then a challenge. Then an insult that old men should have known better than to speak. At that point, the rest of the bar really didn't have any choice but to join in.

Ernie tried to hold back, let some of them get in a punch. But only one. It didn't connect, of course. He moved just before it would have connected, and it hit another man instead. After that, it was a straight-out brawl.

ERNIE TOSSED ANOTHER MAN through Fred, making him cheer.

The ghosts darted through the fighters, distracting people, and generally causing chaos. Except Rab. He was still sitting in the corner with the woman. The only apparent calm in the storm.

There was a faint feeling of electricity in the air. Ernie spun just as the bouncer cracked a man over the head with a cudgel.

'No magic,' the bouncer said, as he nudged the downed man with his foot, then moved back to the door.

Ernie grinned at him, and turned back to the fight, but the few people left conscious wavered on their feet or sat on the floor, looking stunned. No one else came at him. It was disappointing. The brawl had been short-lived, but incredibly efficient. Most of the bar was in pieces, and the old wooden tables and chairs were nothing more than scrap wood. The floor was slick with more than just beer.

'I never knew you had it in you, Ernie. I'm impressed,' Rab said, holding out a hand to help the pretty woman over a broken chair, ignoring the fact neither of them could touch. 'But how is this helping us find Death's Scythe?'

'It's not,' Ernie said, scowling at Rab, irritated with himself. He knew better than to let himself get distracted. 'Anyone who knew anything about the Scythe is long gone now.'

'I saw one in Pierce's vault. He said it was Death's. No one really believed him, of course,' the woman said, stroking the air next to Rab's cheek. The ghostly form rippled. Rab's smile grew. Ernie considered telling Rab what she was but decided against it; she seemed to be helping after all.

'Pierce Waters,' Ernie said with a sigh. Of course, it would be Pierce who had taken it. A collector who liked to layer his house in traps. Great.

Ernie turned to leave, the ghosts following him. As he passed the bouncer, stepping over the man who was still out cold, he couldn't help but ask, 'Are you not paid to prevent this sort of thing?'

'Why? This way, we can send you the bill,' the bouncer said, a small smirk touching his lips as he leaned back against the wall. 'I warned you before you entered.'

Ernie scowled at him, but said nothing as he walked away. Bloody ghosts.

GETTING INTO PIERCE'S HOUSE had been easy, so much so that the ghosts were whispering loudly that Pierce had set a trap for whatever stupid fool broke in. Their top bet was wild dogs ripping Ernie to pieces. In a vain hope of getting them to shut up, he finally triggered a trap for them.

The massive skeleton of a two-headed dog landed on the floor with a clatter. The bones were stark white, still whole and connected, regardless of the fact there was no muscle or fat to hold them there. The trap door it had fallen from swung back and forth, creaking loudly. Dust floated through the ghosts, making them flicker.

'That was it?' Fred said. He tried to tap the thick-boned skeleton with his foot, but it went through. 'Did they forget to feed it?'

The other ghosts sniggered, except for Rab, who was still upset that the woman from the bar had stayed outside. He just grunted.

Ernie stepped over the skeleton and said nothing. If the beast wanted to pretend to be dead, that was alright by Ernie. The thing had made enough noise landing that if Pierce hadn't known they were here before, he would know now.

The ornately carved door at the end of the corridor was, Ernie hoped, where Pierce stored his collections. As they reached it, Pierce opened the door with an exaggerated flourish, then posed as if waiting for a camera crew to take photos.

He wore layers of scarlet semi-transparent gauze tied at his shoulder like a toga. Ernie fervently hoped he had something on under it.

After a minute of silence where even the ghosts had been rendered speechless, or blind, by Pierce's entrance, he turned to them. He hesitated, mouth open, as he looked at them one by one. Then he caught sight of the dog.

'Rus!' Pierce's voice made Ernie wince as he ran to the skeleton. 'What did you do to the poor thing?'

Ernie glared at the beast, which slowly raised its head, eyeless sockets not looking at Ernie as it nuzzled into

Pierce's neck. The coward did not even have the decency to look ashamed.

'It's alive?' Fred asked, peering closer, passing one hand through the beast's ribs. 'But why doesn't it fall apart?'

'Don't do that.' Pierce waved his hand at Fred, but it did little to deter him as he poked his hand through one of the beast's jaws. The dog whined pathetically.

'That's amazing. Where does the sound come from?' Rab said, moving closer.

'Fr—'

'Ernie,' Ernie said, cutting him off before Pierce could use Ernie's real name.

Pierce gritted his teeth, pulling the dog closer. 'Make them stop.'

'Ahh, if only it was that easy. Unfortunately, Death has decided not to collect their souls at this time,' Ernie said.

Rab smiled at Ernie. Then, slowly, with deliberate emphasis, he put his entire head inside the dog's rib cage.

'Death's done what?' Pierce waved his hand through Rab fast enough that the edges of his ghostly form blurred. Rab laughed, repeating the move with less dexterity to Pierce.

'He's rather upset that someone took his Scythe.'

Pierce stopped mid-wave, turning to Ernie. 'Scythe?'

'Yes, someone stole it. Death's under the impression that it might have been me. However, I had nothing to do with it.'

'I didn't steal his Scythe,' Pierce said, but his eyes moved to the door that was still open at the end of the hall.

'Oh well, looks like the ghosts will have to stay longer then,' Ernie said, half turning away.

'Wait,' Pierce shouted as the beast whined again, bones scraping on the floor as it tried to inch away from the ghosts. 'I might have what you're looking for.'

ERNIE PATTED PIERCE'S SHOULDER as they left the house, shifting the Scythe carefully so he didn't hit anyone. The dog had stayed inside.

Pierce sighed, staring at the Scythe with longing. 'It was mine, fair and square.'

'You're welcome to keep it, and the ghosts as well. They loved Rus,' Ernie said, half handing the Scythe back to him just as Rab's voice grew louder.

'I wrestled him to the ground. If not for my actions, the beast would have torn off Ernie's face,' Rab said, chest puffed out as he spoke to the woman from the bar. She listened to Rab's story with wide-eyed fascination.

'No. Take them and do not bring them back,' Pierce said sharply, then frowned at the woman. 'Does he know what she is?'

Fred and the other ghosts were nodding emphatically, supporting Rab's retelling of events, which now included a daring dive through a trap infested corridor. The woman smiled coyly at them, saying very little.

Ernie shrugged. 'No.' The ghosts would all be leaving soon, so it wouldn't matter. At least, that was the plan.

'Don't take this the wrong way, Ernie. Don't visit again soon,' Pierce said, then closed the door in his face.

'What next?' Fred said, pulling away from the others. 'We can go back and teach him a lesson if you like?'

'No,' Ernie said quickly. Fred looked disappointed. 'It's time to visit Death.'

'The rude one from earlier?' Fred said, glancing at the others, who had stopped to watch Ernie. 'We're ready for that one.'

Ernie looked at the four of them, old, gnarled and grumpy. He wasn't sure precisely what Fred thought he was going to do, but the thought of them taking on Death made him smile.

DEATH'S HOUSE WAS QUIET as Ernie entered. The ghosts stayed outside to cheer up Rab, who was saying goodbye to the woman from the bar. Ernie was firm in the belief that no one needed to see that. He winced faintly at the idea of it.

Sitting in front of an open fireplace, which had not been there the last time Ernie had visited, Death still looked distinctly average. He was hunched over a book that had no title; face angled towards the unlit fire. Given the grey tone of everything else, Ernie was glad. It might have been challenging to explain colourless fire to the ghosts.

'Your Scythe,' Ernie said, making Death jump. He turned to stare at the Scythe in Ernie's hand. 'I didn't take the damned thing, but I found who did.'

'I... Well... That is to say...' Death stumbled over the words, standing, and shoving the book on the chair behind him, face turning pink. 'That's not the Scythe.'

'Of course it is,' Ernie said, tilting it so that the light sparked off it, the metal glowing with the magic Death had put in its creation.

'Well, yes, it is one of my Scythes.' He winced. 'But it's not the missing Scythe.'

Ernie stared at him.

'I lost that one in a bet. But he cheated, or I would never have lost it,' Death said, speaking a little too quickly. Pierce, surprisingly, had not been lying for once.

'Well, this is the only one you're bloody getting,' Ernie said. 'I didn't steal your Scythe.'

'—Ah, right. Yes. Of course not.' Death squirmed, shifting his feet on the grey-tiled floor, making a faint squeaking sound. 'I misplaced it.'

'You what?' Ernie asked, somehow sure he must have misheard.

'I misplaced it.' Death moved a little to the side. Leaning against the fireplace was a Scythe, identical to the one in Ernie's hand.

'So, you're telling me you left me with not one but four ghosts, because you forgot where you put your Scythe?' Ernie said slowly.

'Ghosts?' Death said faintly, looking past him. Fred chose that moment to peek around the edge of the door. 'Oh.'

RAB WAS THE LAST to enter Death's house, leaving the woman from the bar outside. He looked a little pale as he approached Ernie.

'You could have told me,' Rab said, shuddering as he looked at the others standing next to Death. 'You won't tell them?'

'That she was a Lamia?' Ernie said. 'You don't have any flesh for her to eat.'

'That doesn't make it OK,' Rab said with a growl.

Ernie gave him his best innocent look as Fred walked over to join them. Rab scowled at both of them as he walked toward Death.

'Some people have too much pride. He could have just told you he found it,' Fred said, joining Ernie to watch the others go.

Ernie snorted.

'It's been fun, though,' Fred added, grinning.

'It's been something,' Ernie replied. He was not sad to see the ghosts go. Not really.

'Why do you stay in that place? I am sure a God could do better,' Fred said, half watching Death as he waited impatiently for Rab to finish his story. It now included a skeleton dog with three heads that was the size of a large horse, a rescue, and a near-death experience that Rab single-handedly prevented.

'Who told you I was a God?' Ernie asked sharply, surprised at Fred's casual tone.

'There was a little man at the bar,' Fred replied. 'He said you were some big shot God. He was less polite. Freda, fryer, something like that.'

'Freyr,' Ernie corrected, wincing at the garbled version of his name. 'Why wouldn't I stay at the Gard Village? I'm old, I'm retired.'

'Gods retire?' Fred, who never had particularly wanted to retire himself, sounded a little confused by the idea.

'I did.'

'I might not know much, but I am pretty sure that's not how it works.'

'I'm a God. It will work however I want it to.'

'You're hiding,' Fred declared. 'You must be. That's the only reason someone would choose a retirement home. Something's coming, something big.'

Ernie scowled at him; he was far too close to the truth. 'I'm not hiding.'

Death coughed loudly. Waving his Scythe. Fred was the last ghost left.

Fred nodded, smiling widely as he moved closer to Death. 'I wish I could have been here to see it.'

'I'm not hiding,' Ernie said, but the Scythe had already swung, and Fred disappeared with a smile on his lips.

THE RETIREMENT HOME WAS a little too quiet when Ernie returned. The general sense of loss had tempered even the lively Betty.

Ernie went to his room, closing himself in. He took the little hourglass he had stolen from Death out of his pocket. It weighed hardly anything. It was hard to believe that this would be the tipping point when the last grains fell.

He carefully put it on its side behind a book in the bookcase. Staring at it for a moment, he made sure the sands were not moving. Then, with care, he put a book in front of it.

The sands of time would not be held back forever, but it would give him a little longer here.

He sighed, remembering Fred's words. He was not hiding; but he knew he was just delaying the inevitable. The last grain would still fall, eventually. But he had time yet before that happened

In The Cards

Author's Notes

I always remember a story my sister told me. It was the middle of winter; snow was falling, and it was bitterly cold outside. She'd been out on the high street with friends. One of them had turned to her and said with a laugh. 'There is always one.'

'One what?' my sister asked.

'An old man wearing shorts.'

My sister followed her gaze. Sure enough, in the centre of the crowd, there was an old man wearing shorts. He was also wearing a woolly hat and a thick jacket. None of which was stopping his legs from turning blue.

That was our granddad. Shorts in winter.

When someone is gone, and all we have is memories, these are the pieces that stick with us.

In The Cards

Ernie leaned across the table, lowering his voice. 'You can't stay here, Fin.'

Fin lifted her eyes slowly to glare at him. 'Don't be ridiculous.'

'Fin—'

A spark of lightning lit the air between them. The magic tingled over his skin like oil on water; there, but not sinking beyond the surface. He waved it away with irritation.

'No magic,' Ernie said. He glanced at the small group of pensioners at the table across the room. At this time of day, the retired residents of Gard Village—Senior Living were playing poker. No one would risk looking away to give Betty the chance to switch a card, so none of them had noticed anything strange. 'Not here.'

'It was just a spark.' Fin rolled her eyes at him, then hesitated as a tiny curl of smoke wove towards the ceiling. She flushed as the smoke grew darker.

Ernie unclenched his teeth with effort as he stomped on the small flame. The bile green carpet was so old and worn that the small burn barely showed. The smell of singed nylon tickled his nose.

'This is my home. I'd rather you didn't burn it down.'

'Don't be rude. I'm a guest,' Fin said as she flicked her grey hair over her shoulder. Not the pale grey of old age, but a gunmetal grey. Her face had thin lines that might have been wrinkles, except they were too regular, and not deep enough.

Ernie imagined this was how a child would have drawn a pensioner. Fin even pressed one hand to her back, groaned in pain, then sat back up straight in her chair with a smile.

'You don't look old enough,' Ernie said at last. He slowly leaned back in his chair like it hurt, even though it didn't.

'I look fantastic,' Fin said. Her image wavered, and the form of a younger woman appeared for a heartbeat. 'Cara would be jealous of how good I look.'

'This is a retirement home, not a meeting of middle-aged housewives.' Ernie pointed to the poker table. He ignored the mention of Cara for now, though it might explain why Fin was here. 'You're supposed to look like them.'

Fin stared at the mixed group of humans who had yet to notice her. They were all over eighty with grey hair, leathery skin, backs stooped forward as they squinted at their cards.

Slowly, Fin's face grew additional lines, and her shoulders sagged as she hunched forward. It was better, if not by much. It had taken Ernie months to get the details right, the wispy hair, and mottled skin. The shuffle.

'There,' Fin said, pushing her chair back without waiting for a response. She turned to the poker table just as Betty squealed in delight. Another win.

'No.' He grumbled too low for anyone at the table to hear him. He probably should not, in hindsight, have pointed Fin towards the poker players. In another time and place, others had made this same mistake. 'No tricks. Not here.'

'You're not being a good host,' Fin said under her breath, but she was smiling as she sat down at the poker table. 'May I join you for a game?'

'We would love another player, my dear,' Albert said, smiling widely at Fin as he straightened his shirt. 'Betty, give the lady some chips.'

'Ha. Of course, you want me to give up some of mine. I'm winning,' Betty said, though she slid a generous stack across to Fin with a wink. 'We put it all back in the pot at the end. We just track who has the most at the end of each game.'

'This is going to be fun,' Fin said, winking at Ernie as she touched the chips.

Somehow Ernie doubted her idea of fun was the same as his.

'You feelin' confident, Albert?' Betty asked, grinning at him over her cards. She was just the other side of eighty, but had the energy of someone far younger.

Albert tapped his cards on the table, not giving away anything about his hand as he raised his eyebrow at Betty. There were only three of them left in the game. Fin had dropped out early, and Ernie had stayed out of it entirely. He didn't like to lose.

'Oh, Betty, Albert is confident,' Jerry said, as he scratched his balding head. 'He's confident that you're cheating.'

They all laughed, Albert included. Betty never lost. Everyone knew it going in. It was one of the inevitable facts of retirement: aching joints, absent grandchildren and Betty cheating at cards.

'Outrageous.' Betty flicked her hair over her shoulder; the silvery curls bounced, drawing the eye away from her hand that quickly switched another card from the ones in her sleeve.

Fin smiled widely as she caught it as well. The move would do little to help Betty with whatever outcome Fin had decided on. Ernie could feel the magic stir the air as Fin placed the next community card. It buzzed around them and pulsed into the fingers of the remaining players.

'Fin—'

'How about we up the stakes?' Fin said, not allowing him to finish. The table rippled with excitement, a slow ripple as their joints creaked, but a ripple, nonetheless. 'Whoever wins this game gets a romantic dinner for two?'

'Romantic? At eighty, we're lucky to eat our meal whole. Mashing your dinner to slurry doesn't really create an amorous atmosphere.' One of the players who had already run out of chips laughed, looking sideways at Betty.

'A night like you were still in your twenties, then. Dance, eat, love, be merry.' Fin laughed as she gave Ernie a knowing look. She was, if nothing else, predictable. 'A carefree and denture free evening.'

'Someone else is paying for dinner? I'm in,' Albert said, shoving half his chips in. Betty followed his lead. The third player shook his head and folded his hand. It was down to just the two now.

'All in,' Albert said, pushing all his chips forward, winking at Fin. If he won now, he would have more than Betty.

Betty opened her mouth, glancing at Albert for a split second, then she folded her hand. 'Too rich for my blood.'

Albert whooped, standing to do a slow jig. His beige shorts showed off his thin, bony knees. He looked more than a little unsteady as he stopped, taking a few wheezing breaths. After he recovered, he tipped his imaginary hat to Betty, who looked far too pleased considering she had lost. 'My lady, would you care to join me this evening?'

She squealed—it was more a screech; even as a young woman, her voice had not been delicate—then smiled widely, taking his hand as she stood. Magic stirred, flowing over the two of them. They stopped, staring at each other. Ernie sighed, waited, but neither said anything.

'Go, enjoy your evening,' Fin said, breaking the silence while motioning to the door. She handed them a small black playing card with writing embossed on one side. 'Take this, and they will give you a meal on the house.'

Everyone gave a little cheer as they followed them as if they were a married couple leaving at the end of the night. Only with walking sticks and slippers as they shuffled. Fin started picking up the remaining cards.

Ernie placed his hands over Betty's, stopping Fin from collecting them. She huffed at him, but he turned them over. They were the winning hand. Fin had fed it to her, and Betty had passed on it.

'You look surprised?'

He hesitated, then gave her the cards, saying nothing. There was a trick, something he wasn't seeing. 'How long will they see the illusion?'

'Just for the night. The best magic is the kind that is short-lived. It's more precious that way.' She smiled as Albert and Betty left. Amazingly, none of the nurses rushed to stop them.

'What happens when they try to do something they aren't fit for?' Ernie asked, wincing as Albert jumped and tried to click his heels, only to stumble a little instead. 'When they realise they are not twenty?'

'I'm not their babysitter, Ernie. It's only an illusion. What they do with it is up to them.'

Ernie cursed as Fin walked away from him. It was going to be a long bloody night.

ERNIE FOLLOWED THE COUPLE. The restaurant was a short distance from the retirement home. Albert walked down the snowy streets with Betty on his arm. He had made one concession to the cold weather: he'd worn his woolly hat. He had not swapped out his shorts, and his legs had taken on a blue tinge that might have worried a less hardy man.

A handful of bars lined the street, their bright neon lights creating a colourful stain on cobblestones despite the fact the afternoon sunlight was hours from disappearing.

Ernie followed them at a distance, making sure that neither could see him. Though the street was generally safe, the cold had driven all the sensible people indoors, leaving only the stupid, or the drunk.

Two men huddled outside the last bar seemed to fit both categories with a cigarette in one shaking hand, the other tucked under an armpit in a vain attempt to keep warm.

The taller of the two was wearing a thin leather jacket, with a tight tank top underneath. He had the build for it, muscles like an anchor's chain, and a thick bull neck.

'Who wears shorts in this weather?' the smaller man said.

'He's probably senile,' the taller of the two said, shouting, as he nudged his friend. 'Lady, you're headed the wrong way. Mental ward's over there.'

'Good one, Bale,' his friend said. They both puffed out a cloud of smoke as they laughed.

At this point, Ernie was sure that Albert would have kept walking, regardless of age or the weather. He was a turn the other cheek sort of guy. Betty was not.

'Big words from a little man, especially as you cower in your corner there,' Betty said as she dragged Albert to a stop.

A small group of women, far better wrapped up for the cold, came out and lit up cigarettes, chatting quietly, glancing between Betty and the men.

'Screw you, lady,' Bale said, stepping closer, flicking a glance at the women. He puffed out his chest, showing off. Not a good sign. 'I dare you to say that again.'

'You're a coward.' Betty grabbed Albert's arm, dragging him forward a step. 'Albert here is a world-class boxer; he will knock your palooka arse on the ground.'

It was almost true, Ernie supposed. Albert had almost been a championship boxer. He had been seconds from a knockout in the first round. Unfortunately, his dodge was never quite as good as his uppercut. A broken jaw later, he was out permanently; never quite reaching fame. He still had some of that grace from his youth, more today for the confidence that the illusion gave him.

'Here, old man, you have the first shot for free,' Bale said as he stepped closer to Albert, sending a smile and a wink toward the women.

Albert shook his head as he moved into a fighter's stance. Bale grinned wider. When Albert swung his fist, he used all the skill he had learned in his youth. But while he might have felt twenty, he was still an old man. Confidence and skill alone would not stop Bale from breaking him.

Just before the punch connected, Ernie closed his own fist tightly. Magic tingled down his fingers.

Bale flew off his feet, hitting the pub wall hard before he slid to the street, unconscious. There was a moment of silence, then the women cheered. Bale's friend dropped his cigarette as he stared at Albert, unable to speak.

'We should get going, my love,' Albert said, putting one arm out for her to hold. He put the other behind his back, stretching it like it hurt. 'We don't want to be late.'

Betty took it with a delighted laugh.

Ernie grinned, tipping his hat to the women as he followed. Bale would probably be fine; the broken jaw would heal. Maybe he would learn manners while it did.

ALBERT AND BETTY STUMBLED into Gard Village, giggling like teenagers caught out late. Ernie waited for them to disappear down the corridor before he followed them in. He was cold and tired. Betty knew how to find trouble, or maybe more accurately, start trouble. The waiter would never be the same, but the fire had not been Ernie's fault.

He was ready to be done with the day, but it wasn't to be. The utter quiet was his first hint that something wasn't quite right. Normally someone was lingering about, even this late. He shouldn't have left Fin alone.

The lights were dim in the communal living room. One of the local doctors and a nurse sipped from two small porcelain teacups. The air was thick with the scent of lavender. Magic stirred faintly as the two stared at each other, not seeing him at all.

'Fin.' Ernie all but growled her name.

'Aren't they cute? They have wanted to be with each other since they first met, but neither dared to find out if the other liked girls.' Fin sighed, eyes growing misty.

'You cannot go around pairing up everyone you see here like a damn cupid on crack.'

'Destiny needs a shove occasionally.' She paused. 'Also, I am not a baby flying around in a nappy, though I could find one if that would make you happier?'

'No, you're the Goddess of forbidden love, Lofn. Neither of these are exactly forbidden.'

Her lips thinned as he used her true name. 'That Betty has quite a shine for you. I could give her a little nudge your way. If that would make you happy?' she said, ignoring his comment entirely.

'What do you want?' Ernie asked as he gave her suggestion the response it deserved. Like he could not win Betty on his own if he wanted. Stupid child.

'Your sister said you were probably bored with all these mortals and could use the company,' Fin said, sighing as she glanced at the couple again.

The two women reached for each other, trying to go through the table rather than around it. Both cups fell off, one somehow landing upright while the other spilt pale water across the floor as it bounced along the carpet.

'Bored? I am not bored. Fr—' He cut off before he said his sister's name. Having her pop in as well would not help to keep her out of his damn business.

'I want to make other people happy. Is that so much to ask?' Fin's words were sharp as she ignored him. 'Cara is wrong.'

At the mention of Fin's long-term girlfriend, Ernie cringed. 'Where is Cara?'

'She said we're done. Fine, we're done. I don't care where she is,' Fin said, turning away from him.

'Fin—'

'I've moved on. Love at first sight? Ha. Love takes work, and it takes bravery to act on it. I'll show her. Just you watch me.' It was more of a threat than the sentiment deserved.

The doctor moaned as the nurse pulled her towards a door at the back of the room. Several pieces of clothes littered the ground behind them. When Ernie turned back, Fin was gone.

Damned Goddesses of love could fix everything but their own love life. He would not spend the next decade fixing her idea of 'love'.

He knew of only one way to get rid of her when she was like this.

ERNIE DODGED THE LIGHTNING bolt Cara threw at him. Heat sizzled by his face a second before the lamp behind him exploded. He didn't say Lofn's name again.

The air buzzed with unleashed lightning as Cara gathered more energy. Her once white dress floated around her. She hesitated, eyes streaming with tears, then let the bolt fizzle out. The smell of ozone was thick in the air as she collapsed, sobbing like she was the one who'd been attacked.

Ernie hesitated. Cara had already taken her anger out on the now mostly destroyed room. Fragments of glass and wood covered the floor. But that wasn't why he hesitated.

He was of the firm belief that someone crying should be left to themselves until the snot, tears, and—in the case of Gods—the lightning had ceased.

That took time.

Cara and Fin's fights were notorious. He didn't have the years it could take for the pair of them to make-up.

'I hate her,' Cara spat. Her hair hung around her face in a lank brown tangle.

Ernie skirted wide of a broken table, waving away static as the air sparked. 'Now I doubt that,' Ernie said, crouching next to her. He kept his face smooth at the glare she levelled at him. 'You should talk to her.'

'Never.' She threw herself at him without warning, clinging to him like a damp limpet. He winced, patting her back like he'd seen others do.

'She says she exaggerated. She didn't mean it,' Ernie said, grasping at something that was probably true. It seemed to help. The tears slowed, at least.

'She exaggerated?' The words were muffled in his shoulder.

Ernie glanced at what had once been a set of wine glasses, the stems the only part still intact among the small shards of glass, and he had a distinct but brief image of his home in a similar state. While the outdated furniture was mostly worn, old and uncomfortable, he did not want to see it destroyed. 'Yes. She said she takes it back.'

'About love?' Cara pulled back, blinking tears away as she stared at him, head tilted slightly to one side.

'Sure. She takes it back,' Ernie said, keeping the expression from his face, hoping that what he was saying would continue to work.

'What did she say, exactly?' Cara leaned back further, letting him go. He tried to wipe the snot from his shoulder without her noticing. There really was not any need to be quite this human.

'That she loves you,' he said slowly, watching to see if that was the right thing to say. She barely blinked at him, but the static tingled against his skin.

'Nothing else?'

He hesitated. Cara pushed herself to her feet, stepping back onto broken glass. It melted rather than broke. Maybe this was not going as well as he had thought. 'Tell me what she said.'

Ernie opened his mouth, but Cara didn't wait for him to answer.

'No, no. I have a better idea,' Cara said, smiling slowly. 'I'll ask her.'

She took another step back, disappearing between one breath and the next. Ernie cursed. That did not sound like it was going to go well.

As Ernie stepped inside the retirement home, the hairs on his arms danced.

Fin was lounging on the sofa, still in her old woman form, wearing a large jumper and furry slippers.

Cara stood in the middle of the room, lightning flickering between her fingers as she stared at Fin. In the time it had taken them to get there, Cara's dress was clean, and her hair was flowing over her shoulder in a healthy wave of brown.

'Sjöfn,' Ernie said, using Cara's full name carefully. She ignored him.

A low moan stopped him from continuing. He stared at the windows around the nurse's station. They had steamed up like he was stuck in the scene from the Titanic, despite the fact it was neither cold enough nor damp enough for it to have happened naturally. Fin didn't even have the decency to look embarrassed as he raised an eyebrow at her. She continued to glare at Cara.

'Cara is not welcome here.' Dismissive did not come close to describing her tone.

Ernie considered retreating at that point. He might even have made it, though it was probably unlikely. He was, however, reluctant to abandon his home to them. He was comfortable here.

'I—' Ernie tried to talk, but Cara cut him off.

'Ernie said that you wanted to apologise for what you said to me,' Cara said.

Fin shot him a dark look, and he decided it was probably better to say nothing.

'Love at first sight...' Fin said, giving an exaggerated wave at the steamed-up windows as she stood, '...is a lie. They didn't love each other at first sight, or they wouldn't have waited three years before hooking up.'

'You don't know that. You were not there when they met. It might have just taken time—'

'That's not love at first sight.' Fin almost shouted as she stepped forward. The carpet squelched as her foot landed in the spilt tea. The scent of lavender flooded the air as it slowly soaked into her slipper.

'I loved you the first time I saw you,' Cara said, stepping closer, accidentally kicking the other teacup that was still upright. It rolled over next to its twin, splashing the pale liquid over her bare feet. The smell of lavender grew stronger, and the lightning dissipated from Cara's fingers. 'How could you not feel the same way?'

'I...' Fin stared at Cara.

Tears hovered at the edge of falling as Cara waited for Fin to finish. Ernie was not sure which part of this he hated worse: the tears, or the possible destruction. He almost wished they would fight.

'The first time you spoke to me,' Fin whispered.

'What?'

'I fell in love with you the first time you spoke to me.' Fin stepped closer, taking Cara's hands in hers. 'You smiled and laughed at something I said.'

'You never told me that before.' Cara looked down at Fin's hands in hers.

'I always thought you knew,' Fin said, pulling Cara close, kissing her.

Ernie released the breath he had been holding as he turned away to give them privacy.

Damn love Goddesses. Lust, or love, first sight, or slow burn. Did it really matter? They were making it far too complicated. He wasn't smiling.

NOW THAT CARA AND Fin were back together, neither wanted to linger. They had gone outside to say goodbye. Until Fin's tea wore off, it was going to be a little awkward in the communal living room.

'I think I see it, the appeal of living here,' Fin said, smiling at Cara, who was lazily writing 'Mid' in the snow that had stuck to the Gard Village—Senior Living's sign. 'It's quiet.'

'You were never very good with quiet, Lofn,' Ernie said, deciding not to mention that it had not been quiet in any way since Fin had arrived. He hoped that as the morning rolled round, the magic of the night before would be over. Things would go back to quiet.

Fin looked behind her, where they could see the silhouettes of Albert and Betty dancing in one of the windows. 'I guess I have never been good with silence. Freya doesn't like that you're here, you know.'

'Yes, my sister has made that very clear.' Ernie winced as he remembered their last argument. He should not have been surprised that she had sent Fin his way when the opportunity had presented itself.

'She will not leave you alone until you leave this place,' Fin said, shaking her head at him, growing serious.

'She is nothing if not persistent,' Ernie said with a sigh.

'Freyr, you know you can't stay here forever; the wheels have already started turning.' He winced as she used his full name.

'I know, but they aren't in place yet,' he said, looking at the sky. He had time yet. For now, he was free, and he was going to enjoy the peace while it lasted.

A Genie's Day Off

Author's Notes

I can't remember my granddad without a beard. More often than not, it was long and scraggly, like Santa on a bad day. But there was always one other constant with it: there always seemed to be food buried in it somewhere. Or maybe it's just a constant of old men with beards.

If it was ever pointed out—and it regularly was—his first answer was always, 'I'm saving it for later,' which goes a long way to tell you what kind of man my granddad was.

It's probably tainted my view of beards forever, but it's a memory that will not soon be forgotten.

A Genie's Day Off

Ernie waved away the puff of green smoke as it tried to choke him.

'Go away,' he muttered under his breath, refusing to be chased out of his chair. The smoke ignored him as it continued to writhe uncomfortably close to his skin; the magic making his senses tingle.

Ernie gritted his teeth and did a quick check of the room; no one else had noticed the smoke. Probably because Gard Village—Senior Living was having the seasonal rush that was Mother's Day. Children arrived en-mass as they remembered their elderly relatives they had tucked away in a home out of sight. The room overflowed with people, most clustered in groups on old, mismatched furniture.

Ernie didn't normally get visitors, and certainly not on Mother's Day. It had been the point of living in a retirement home, in the body of an eighty-year-old. This visitor was especially unwelcome.

The smoke tugged at him. It was only a matter of time before someone noticed. With a grunt, he pushed himself out of the chair. 'This had better be good.'

The smoke dropped to swirl around his ankles like a giant green snake, disappearing and reforming with every step he took. One of the visitors glanced at him, blinking rapidly at the smoke, then looked away. Denial. Such a useful human state of mind.

Ernie waited until he had left the communal living room before he spoke again. 'I don't have all day.'

The smoke spooled out and upwards, then between one step and the next, a tall man in his twenties was walking beside Ernie. The man was almost six feet tall, with the toned body of someone who spent just a hair too much time on how he looked. Or at least he would have if he'd been human.

'You do have all day. Since you're retired, time is all you have,' John said, smiling as he jogged ahead, then turned to walk backwards in front of Ernie.

'John.' Ernie gave him a warning glare.

John smiled again, green eyes sparkling. 'I need a favour.'

'No.' Ernie shook his head to emphasise.

'You don't know what the favour is.' John's smile got wider.

'I don't have to. I already know I'm not interested.' Ernie didn't have to know the specifics to know it would go wrong. John was like a natural disaster that way.

'I need someone to cover for me. Just for a few days.'

'Cover?' Ernie stopped. The quiet stretch of hallway led to the private rooms of the residence. Those that were not out front with the rest were too deaf to hear them.

'I have a date,' John said, looking away shyly.

Ernie was not the sentimental sort. The words in no way swayed his decision on the matter. And yet he did not repeat the no.

'Chances are there will be nothing interesting. I might not even get called.'

Chances were like the weather. No one could predict them accurately. Ernie should have known better.

'One day,' Ernie said, huffing a breath as John patted him on the shoulder.

'You won't regret this,' John said. He turned, then shouted over his shoulder. 'Don't forget the rules.'

'What rules?' Ernie asked. A tiny puff of green smoke hovered in the air where John had been. Ernie spat out the taste of chocolate, shuddering. There were far less disgusting ways to use magic.

Ernie exhaled slowly. He should have said no.

ERNIE RE-JOINED THE SELECTION of seasonal well-wishers, watching as various middle-aged men and women made their excuses to leave. The man who had seen the smoke looked at him with relief, the denial working hard.

'It's always so nice to see you, Eugene,' Betty said as she hugged a hefty man in his late fifties. Grey hair and receding hairline, twin chins half hidden by a beard, and a belly that Betty could have sat on.

'I would come more often, mother,' he replied, patting her awkwardly. 'Things are just so busy now at work.'

'I understand,' Betty said, sounding sincere. Ernie knew it to be a lie. The clock had started ticking on how long it would take her to explode like an overripe melon hitting the ground. Her son never noticed.

Betty waved goodbye, then caught Ernie's eye. Something flashed in her hand, and her expression turned sad. By the time her son had left the building, she was grinning and rolling a man's gold watch around in her hands. Age had not made those fingers any less agile.

'What did he get?' Ernie asked her.

She raised an eyebrow at him, touching her silver hair that was piled in a bun. Age had done little to diminish its length and volume; much to her pleasure.

Ernie said nothing, and she eventually sighed, and began checking her own jewellery and trinkets.

'Nothing's missing?' Betty sounded disappointed. Worse, she sounded sad, deflated. 'Maybe he really is busy?'

'Maybe it's something you haven't missed yet?' Ernie ventured. The room was almost empty of people now. Betty murmured something and shuffled away. It was not like her to give in so easily.

Ernie turned to take a step towards her, then stopped as the room turned to smoke around him.

It took him a minute to realise that it wasn't the room that had changed; it was him.

Ernie cursed as the smoke held him tight.

THE SMOKE SPAT ERNIE out in a burst of light.

Ernie liked to think it had let him go because of his threat to tear apart the essence of the smoke until it was nothing more than space dust. Unfortunately, it looked like they had just arrived at their destination.

With a barely audible thwack, Ernie landed on his feet on an unfamiliar floor. He had not fallen very far, at least.

He glared at the smoke as he brushed himself off. John's magic seemed confused by the reaction; its wispy smoke form darted around the room erratically, as if to provide an explanation.

Ernie followed its motion, taking in the slightly chaotic space. The outer walls were made from sloping panels of distorted glass; none were the same size or shape, but they all flowed towards a point in the ceiling. Light and colour danced across it in patterns that had little effect on the light in the room itself.

The space was split into sections—bedroom, kitchen and what might have been a bathroom—by a series of bookcases that acted as walls. Each one looked to be double-sided and filled to bursting with hand bound books and older scrolls.

One particularly large book stood apart from the rest, sitting on a wooden plinth. It had a bright pink post-it note stuck to the front. 'No lawyers.'

Before Ernie could explore further in the traditional fashion of those left alone unattended in the house of strangers, the walls shuddered.

He froze, ready to brace or duck for cover, but nothing else moved. A patch of light appeared in a clear space in the centre of the room. It came from a circular opening in the ceiling that had not been there a moment before.

'No,' Ernie said, glaring at it. He was so focused on the patch of light he didn't see the trail of smoke sneaking up behind him until it was too late.

He was ripped from the floor in a rush of smoke, light, and colour. 'Not again,' he tried to mutter, but the words were lost.

There was a sensation of being squished too small, and stretched too thin, then he landed with a thump as his arse hit the cold wood floor. The smoke tried to hold on, clinging like a beetle to his skin, but Ernie forced it back, sending it spinning away a step. It immediately started back towards him.

'No,' Ernie said. The single word made the smoke hesitate. It retreated, confused and anxious, like it was the one who had been wronged.

'You're—' A familiar man's voice sputtered the word a few times, then got stuck.

Ernie sighed, and got up slowly, managing not to stand on the small prism shaped bottle that he had just been inside by sheer force of will. The smoke's. It rolled the bottle out from under Ernie's feet at the last second.

'You can't be real.' Eugene was standing in the centre of his living room. Face red and blotchy as he glanced from the bottle back to Ernie. He had a sandwich in one hand, ketchup had dripped from it onto his beard, he didn't seem to notice.

'Why not? Do I not look like a Genie?' Ernie said, crossing his arms, trying to recover some level of dignity. He was going to kill John when he saw him next.

'Well?' Eugene looked him up and down, clearly unimpressed by Ernie's old man shape.

'Would you rather I wear one of those bikinis? Would that make you happy?' Ernie snapped at him. The smoke sidled closer, hovering near his leg. Ernie turned to it. 'Do it and I will put you back in the bottle.' It pulled back, sulking.

'No—'

'Or perhaps I am the wrong colour, maybe if I was blue?'

'I—'

'Better yet, why don't I cross my arms and give you an exaggerated blink? Would that satisfy you?'

'You—'

'I know. How about I float on a patch of smoke? Then I can hang around in the air. Because that surely is more efficient than two legs? I mean, how could that possibly go wrong?'

This time, the man kept his mouth shut. Ernie took a slow breath. 'What do you want?' Ernie managed a moderately even tone.

The tendril of smoke tapped him on the leg. 'No,' Ernie told it firmly. It slunk away from him like a kicked dog. Ernie would not feel bad for it.

'What?' Eugene's voice had raised a pitch.

'What. Do. You. Want?' Ernie repeated slower.

'What can I have?' The man was a little closer to the door than Ernie remembered.

'Whatever you want, it's your wish.' Ernie shrugged, then sighed as the smoke tugged at his leg again. He added cautiously. 'With a few exceptions?'

'You don't sound very sure.' Eugene glanced down at the bottle and back up at Ernie. 'If you want to, you know, go check, or something. I can wait.'

Ernie laughed. He couldn't help it.

It was too much for the man. He bolted for the door like a rabbit, dropping the sandwich in his rush. Ernie let him go.

The smoke hovered disapprovingly around the bottle. Ernie ignored it and headed to the kitchen in search of food while he waited. He didn't think he would have to wait long. Ernie didn't know how John did this all the time. People were strange.

IT DIDN'T TAKE LONG for Eugene to come back. He snuck in as much as his bulk allowed for, trying to move silently.

Ernie pretended not to notice as he ate from the bag of popcorn he'd found. Maybe if he stayed seated at the kitchen table, he wouldn't spook the man. Again. He didn't want to be here all day.

'What are the rules? I mean, what can't I do?' Eugene asked nervously. He was standing in the doorway, sweat beading on his forehead, and his eyes showing more white than was likely healthy.

The smoke vibrated around the bottle like a dog that had been told it was walk time. Ernie sighed, wanting to wave the smoke away, but it was just so desperate to do something. He nodded at it, and it immediately misted inside the bottle, making Eugene jump.

A heartbeat later, a large book appeared roughly a foot above Eugene's hand. He fumbled to catch it, fingers slipping and only just catching the cover. It ripped from the book with a loud shredding sound, followed by a massive thump.

Eugene froze, paling as he glanced at the smoke that had darted clear of the drop and looped itself around Ernie's leg. It undulated uncomfortably against his ankle.

'I'll fix it,' Ernie said softly to the smoke. It held on tighter, quivering. 'He won't even notice it was broken.'

'I'm sorry,' Eugene said. He looked almost as upset as the smoke felt.

'Look, just make a wish.' Ernie pushed the popcorn away and put his full attention on the man. 'If you can't have it, I'll tell you.'

Eugene hesitated, not looking up from the book. The ketchup had smeared into his beard, making it hard to focus on anything else. Ernie considered telling him it was there.

'I wish that no matter how much I ate that I never got fat.' Eugene spoke in a rush. Like he was afraid of the joke to come. He looked up as he finished.

'Ok,' Ernie said. It was a simple thing to do. He was just starting to gather the magic when the smoke tightened around his leg. It was so desperate to help, and after the book, it probably needed the confidence boost.

Ernie sighed, then nodded. He let it wrap itself around the idea of what the man wanted, pouring magic and energy into it. It felt odd working within its limitations, like trying to wear a pair of shoes a size too small.

The wish came together as the smoke expanded and covered Eugene, snapping the magic into place. Then the smoke sprang back into a small circle around Ernie's ankle. It hummed with pleasure.

Eugene coughed, taking a step back, looking down at himself. 'It didn't work?' Eugene asked, touching his stomach.

'Yes, it did,' Ernie said, pushing the leftover popcorn towards him. 'You can eat anything you want.'

Eugene scowled. 'I'm still fat.'

'You didn't ask to lose weight.' Ernie narrowed his eyes, not liking the change from nervous to ungrateful.

'It was implied.'

'I'm not psychic. I gave you what you asked for,' Ernie said, taking the popcorn back, stuffing a handful in his mouth. 'You want to be thin. Wish for that.'

'It's not about being skinny,' Eugene said, as he flexed his fingers that were as big as sausages, then slumped into the other seat at the table. 'My fingers used to be so thin that I could pull a pin from a woman's hair, and she wouldn't even notice until her hair tumbled down. Now. Now, I can barely tie my own shoelaces.'

Ernie didn't ask why Eugene would want to undo women's hair without being noticed. It seemed beside the point, and in Ernie's opinion, likely to annoy people. But the image of Betty always putting her hair up when Eugene visited was suddenly very vivid in Ernie's mind.

'What do you want?' Ernie asked.

'You must think I am shallow. A foolish little fat man who has no self-control.' Ernie did not look at the ketchup.

'I don't think you're small,' Ernie said, face straight. Eugene snorted at him like a horse.

'I wish I was thin,' Eugene said with a shuddering breath.

The smoke barely waited for Ernie's approval before it moved. Changing how someone looked was no small piece of magic, as the energy was more this time. The smoke covered Eugene, hiding the progress. But when Eugene's pants fell to the floor, Ernie was pretty sure it had worked.

IT WAS IMPOSSIBLE NOT to be impressed by the change. Eugene, it turned out, was not half bad looking when he was skinny. Delicate cheekbones, and large wide eyes gave him an almost feminine look. Ernie had known Eugene was tall, but now that he was slim, it really put it into perspective. He stretched his long, nimble fingers.

Of course, it might have been more impressive if he wasn't standing in a shirt that was about ten sizes too big and his trousers around his ankles. At least the shirt was long enough that it meant he was mostly decent.

'I've never been this skinny in my life,' Eugene said as he twisted, looking down at himself, dangerously close to flashing. 'Is this real?'

'Do you doubt your own eyes?' Ernie asked, looking away as Eugene twisted the other way a little too quickly, trying to see himself in the shine of the fridge door.

'What do I do now?' Eugene sounded a little panicked.

'Find some pants?' Ernie suggested, keeping his eyes facing the other direction.

'No. No. I have one wish left. Three. They come in threes,' Eugene said, almost desperate. 'I can't waste it.'

'Waste it? You have everything you want, right?' Ernie narrowed his eyes at the man as he grew shifty.

Eugene was staring at the little prism bottle, no longer listening to Ernie. 'Go back in the bottle.'

'No.' Ernie folded his arms, ignoring the tug from the smoke on his leg. 'Like hell I will.'

Eugene wasn't going to take that for an answer. There was a debate, a short flash of indecision that crossed his face, then he dived for the bottle. Ernie should have stopped him. Would have, but he did not want to tackle a half-naked man.

The second Eugene's hands touched the bottle, the smoke's tug became a tornado of force and Ernie was dragged towards the bottle.

Ernie landed on the floor of John's apartment with a curse on his lips.

ERNIE WAS STUCK. NO, that wasn't true. He could break the bottle, but that was rude. So, he was stuck until Eugene let him out or John came home. Right now, that seemed unlikely.

Next time John asked him for a favour, Ernie was going to shove the bottle so far—

Thud.

Ernie turned to stare at the book that had landed on the floor by the bookcase. Its cover lay beside it, moving in small jerking motions as the smoke circled it, trying to put it back together. Ernie sighed, giving up on trying to find a way out. He was not desperate enough to destroy John's home.

The sticky note was once again stuck to the front, curled at the edges like it had been removed and replaced several times. There was too little of the cover's ragged edge left to try to weave it together with the rest of the book. Ernie picked it up, nudging the smoke away. It hovered in a little green puddle beside him.

There had to be some way to attach it back together. Ernie looked around the open space. There were dozens of drawers and storage units, nooks and crannies. Ernie smiled.

John turned out to be a hoarder. Every space was filled with a random collection of stuff. Most of which would have been rubbish to anyone else. After Ernie emptied the fourth drawer on the floor, he started to feel a little guilty. Then he remembered he was stuck and continued. The smoke seemed confused, but happy, to help move things around.

It was hard to tell how long they 'searched'. Time didn't necessarily move the same way inside the bottle, and Ernie had not bothered to check it. Eventually, Ernie stepped back and surveyed his work with a smile.

'I think that looks all right?' Ernie said, nodding at the book, now repaired. Even the post-it note was no longer curling. The smoke gave a little happy swirl as it agreed. He was quite proud of how it turned out.

'Let's—'

Ernie cut off as the little beam of light re-appeared in the centre of the room. Eugene had got bored, it seemed. Ernie nodded to the smoke who circled around him. A scathing whip sharp comment was ready to throw as he reformed outside the bottle.

The comment died on his tongue as the smoke dissipated and he saw Eugene where he lay on the sofa. At least, that's who Ernie thought it was.

'It might be time to get John,' Ernie said quietly to the smoke. It hovered nervously behind his ankle, not willing to get any closer. 'Go fetch him.'

JOHN OPENED AND CLOSED his mouth, staring at Eugene with growing horror. 'What did you do?'

Ernie said nothing. It was hard to take John seriously with the Hawaiian shirt and speedo shorts. But it was better than looking at Eugene.

Eugene groaned, making Ernie wince.

'You're supposed to guide the magic, not let it do what it wants.' John folded his arms and stared at the smoke. It was half hidden behind Ernie's leg, barely a puff of smoke visible. 'There is a reason it needs a host.'

'He wished to be thin. We made him thin,' Ernie said, shifting his feet so John focused on him.

'Thin? He's skeletal. I've seen corpses with more meat,' John shouted, hitting a pitch that grown men should not attempt.

'He didn't start that thin,' Ernie said, unable to stop himself from looking at Eugene. Skeletal was being kind. Every bone showed through paper thin skin where he was laid out on the couch, loosely covered by a blanket. Food scraps surrounded him, and the ketchup was no longer the only thing in his beard.

'What else did he wish for?' John asked, crossing his arms.

'To be able to eat and not gain weight.'

'Are you insane?' John stared at him as if he had already decided the answer.

'The wishes didn't interact well with each other. How was I supposed to know that?'

'People need to do more than eat to survive. Weight change is human biology. You don't change biology.' John took a slow breath. 'You made it so that no matter what he ate, he never gained any nutrients. Never gain any benefits from the food.'

Ernie stared at the fragments of food that covered every surface. Horror rising. 'He would have been forever hungry but never able to satisfy it?'

'Yes,' Eugene's voice was a harsh rasp. His eyes were sunken, pain shone on them.

'He still has one wish left?' John asked.

Ernie nodded.

John waved to the smoke. It moved slowly over to John like a dog who knew it had pissed on the carpet and was in trouble. When it touched John's leg, the smoke grew, swirling, rising in a cyclone until it covered John's legs.

'Show off,' Ernie muttered. John ignored him.

'Wish for me to fix it,' John said quietly, touching the man's shoulder with care.

'Fix me. Wish,' Eugene rasped. Magic surged in response.

Eugene looked at his fingers with a sorrowful expression. 'I know it wasn't worth it. But I miss being thin.' He was back in the clothes he had started with, belly bulging the buttons, and chins dancing behind his beard with every word. The food was still mashed into it.

'I'm sorry it didn't turn out how you expected,' Ernie said.

'I'm sorry about the bottle thing.' Eugene turned away. 'I just panicked.'

'There is a reason Gluttony is a sin, Eugene. Temptation is part of life. Finding balance is not meant to be easy,' Ernie said, trying to sound sage.

John sniggered.

'What happens now?' Eugene said, looking from Ernie to John. 'I mean, does life just go back to normal?'

'That's up to you. I reset things to how they had been before.' John held his prism bottle in one hand and a handful of popcorn in the other. He was sitting on the sofa alone. The smoke had retreated to the bottle now the final wish was done. 'What do you want?'

'I want to make my mum smile again.' The words held a note of confidence that had been lacking before.

John stood, folding the empty popcorn bag, and dumped it on the coffee table. 'Then remember that. It's time for us to go.'

'Thank you,' Eugene said, looking at Ernie.

John gripped Ernie's shoulder, letting the smoke rise in a cloud around them, and settle them back into the quiet corridor at Guard Village—Senior Living.

'When you asked me to cover, you could have warned me your bottle was out in the wild,' Ernie said to John, trying to scrape the taste of popcorn out of his mouth. It was one thing to have eaten it himself. This really was an unnecessary side effect of the magic.

John grunted. 'Next time I'll remember to check.'

'Next time?' Ernie turned to John, a warning halfway forming on his lips, but John was already gone. 'Bloody

Genies,' Ernie muttered as he stalked back to the Communal living room.

IT WAS A FEW weeks later when Ernie saw Eugene again. He was standing with Betty in the communal living room.

'Have you lost weight?' Betty asked, hugging Eugene tightly.

Eugene kissed her cheek and pulled back. He had indeed lost weight, enough that his clothes were loose. 'It's slow going. But it's going the right way.'

Betty stepped back, shaking her head. Her hair fell from its bun, ringlets bouncing down around her. She laughed, touching her hair.

Eugene took her hand gently and placed a pin in it. 'I'm sorry I haven't been a good son recently.'

'You're here,' Betty said, smiling widely as she pulled him into another hug. 'What more can I ask for?'

Eugene looked up at Ernie, smiling. Ernie returned it, then left the two of them alone. Eugene might not have got exactly what he wished for, but it looked like he had got what he wanted.

John dropped the book on the mahogany desk with a thump. Its cover had been taped back together with dozens of rows of kids' plasters. Green dinosaurs and pink elephants danced across them in clashing bright colours.

The room was spacious, with a lot of wood furniture and reds and browns for colour. The woman behind the desk glanced at the book, then went back to looking at the handwritten scroll in her hands.

'Why did you move my bottle?' John asked, tapping the book.

'I don't know what you're talking about,' Freya said. She was a tall woman in her mid-twenties, with vivid red hair that hung in waves down her back. She was a surprisingly bad liar.

'He made a mess,' John said, shoving the book further forward. The post-it note that had been sitting easily removed on top was now taped down with the same plasters. 'You moved the bottle so he would.'

'My brother needs to get out more,' Freya said, smiling. 'It's nice of you to help him do that.'

'Keep me out of your games. Whatever they are.' John picked up the book, managing not to throw it at her.

'He can't stay there forever.' Freya leaned back in her chair, letting the scroll curl closed.

'It's not your choice. Freyr can do whatever the hell he wants, including pretending to be an old man called Ernie in a rundown retirement home.' John smiled as Freya scowled at him. 'It's his choice.'

'The time is almost here.' Freya added weight to those words.

'But it isn't here yet,' John said, turning and walking away before Freya could say more. Damned siblings couldn't talk to each other, and it was people like John, who were left to clean up the mess.

Now he just had to convince his date that he'd abandoned her for a good reason. Joy.

THE WILD HUNT

AUTHOR'S NOTES

MY GRANDAD ALWAYS LIKED to tell stories about how he could fix things—to be fair, he mostly could, even if it might not have been the correct or safest way to do it. He had a lot of varying skills that he had picked up over the years. And of course, he always wanted to help.

He'd help strangers, sometimes over family or friends. He liked to be needed, I think, and wanted to be there for anyone who asked.

But there were also times that he was overly generous with how much he might have contributed to that 'fix'. Starting somewhere around watching while someone worked, until the story morphed over time and it was my granddad who provided the solution and saved the day.

As I wrote this story, I tried to bring the essence of that to Norris and Charles. That passion.

Gone, but not forgotten, and even the wild stories live on.

The Wild Hunt

Death was a fact of life. The fallout from it varied, from grief to pleasure, to rage. Today Ernie was getting to see two of those reactions first hand.

'He lied,' Archie said, voice tight as he wavered from rage back to grief. He sat slumped in his wheelchair, spindly body weak from years without walking. At seventy-five, he was one of the younger residents of Gard Village—Senior Living.

'I'm sure it's just a misunderstanding,' Ernie said, trying to escape the conversation. The communal living room was quiet. Everyone was watching Archie with a sense of kinship, while also staying far enough back that they didn't actually have to deal with it directly.

'He's a cheat,' Archie spat, slipping back to rage as he straightened, the motion sending his chair rolling forward a step. He just caught the wheel before he hit Ernie. 'He promised he would leave them to me.'

There was a general mutter of agreement from the other residents, who were valiantly keeping a distance, avoiding getting directly involved. Ernie glared at them; it had no effect. He wasn't letting the rest of the residents get out of helping that easily.

Ernie opened his mouth, ready to pick a few of them out by name, but before he could, energy tingled over his skin, stopping him. It shouldn't have been there, but something about it felt familiar.

Archie took Ernie's silence as a chance to keep talking. 'We collected those coins together. He betrayed me, Ernie.' Archie slipped back into a slump.

'You should hunt them down and make them pay.' The soft feminine voice drew all eyes and held them. Taller than most men, she would have stood out in any crowd. Add the heavy build that wouldn't have looked wrong on a warrior, and hair so blond it looked silver, Sky commanded attention.

'It's good to see you again, Ernie,' she said, smiling, like she'd been invited.

Ernie sighed. He might not have recognised the twenty-year-old human body, but it didn't make her any less familiar. He hadn't thought this day could get worse.

'Ernie.' Archie pushed himself upright, straightening his wispy hair, then smoothing his shirt. He was not alone; most of the rest of the men followed suit. 'Why don't you introduce your friend?'

'My name's Sky,' she said, tilting her head at Archie in greeting, expression turning serious. 'Do you want to hunt them down?'

'No,' Ernie said, barely waiting for her to finish talking. Everyone ignored him.

Archie preened at the attention. Some of his grief faded as she changed his focus. 'Maybe once, lass,' Archie said, scowling at the chair. 'Who is going to fear me now?'

'Tell me, who's done you wrong?' Sky said, crouching next to the wheelchair. 'Maybe I can help remind them to be afraid?'

The anger crept back into Archie. 'My friend stole from me. Then he died. Left it all to his son.'

'Then we should get back what was stolen?' Magic tingled against Ernie's skin as she spoke the words.

'Absolutely not,' Ernie said. This time, he drew every eye in the room. Like he was the crazy one. He could feel the wild magic giving Archie new strength. Temporary strength. 'That's not a good idea.'

'It is,' Archie said, straightening in his seat. 'I want what is mine. I want to do it.'

'Done,' Sky said, standing, eyes going to Ernie's. 'I love a good hunt.'

'How are we supposed to get there, exactly? Do you even know where the coins are?' Ernie scowled at Sky. This was not how today was supposed to go. It should have been a quiet wake, some biscuits and then lots of old stories with a round of whisky or two.

'You worry too much, Ernie.' Sky smiled, showing teeth. 'I'm sure we can figure all of that out.'

AN HOUR LATER, THEY stood, or in a few cases sat, outside. It was cold and windy, and only three of the residents had braved the weather to join Archie on his journey for vengeance. No one seemed to question why they did not just get a taxi to the person's home.

Archie had upgraded his wheelchair to an electric mobility scooter. The shiny red paint was clean, and the plastic rain covers pulled back. A silver and black horse had been stencilled into the paint. Ernie was sure it hadn't been there before.

'Sky.' Ernie tried to get her attention. She ignored him.

'This is perfect,' Jerry said, stroking the handles of an older version of Archie's scooter. He was a man in his eighties, almost bald, with barely a few wisps of thin, grey hair left. He settled back in the massive seat. It might have once had a frame for a rain shelter, but it had been removed and replaced with a large leather-backed seat that would have looked more at place on a Harley.

Archie and Jerry smiled at each other and nudged the two scooters forward. They buzzed like hairdryers, drowning out much of the other sounds.

'What do I get?' Norris asked, glancing at the other two mobility scooters with a frown. He was a short round man, with a beer belly that had taken decades to perfect.

'You get to be my driver,' Sky said as she smiled at him, indicating to a wire-framed golf caddy that was parked in front of the Gard Village sign. The cart had not been there before, and it had a black dog printed on the side of it. Ernie glared at Sky.

Norris whooped excitedly, then with a quick as shuffle as he could manage, he levered himself inside. He tested the controls, and with a few jerking stop-starts, he drew level with the two mobility scooters.

'This is not a hunt,' Ernie said, grabbing Sky's arm as she passed him.

'We are going to get vengeance for your friend,' Sky said, raising her eyebrow. 'Of course, it's a hunt.'

'You know what I mean, Sky,' Ernie said, keeping his voice low. Though he probably could have shouted and none of the others would have noticed as they fiddled with hearing aids and pulled on woolly hats. 'I want no funny business.'

Sky just smiled, slipping from his grip to step into the cart's second seat. She turned to him, nodding towards the sign. 'I didn't forget about you.'

Beside the sign was a black scooter, not the mobility kind like the others had, but one of those new adults' scooters with two wheels. It was electric, with a wide footrest and handles.

I would have rather ridden a horse, he thought as he huffed a frustrated breath.

But this was not that kind of hunt.

'Unless you don't feel up to the challenge?' Sky said, turning away from him.

Ernie stepped on the scooter with a grunt. Like he was going to leave his people alone with her.

RIDING DOWN THE CENTRE of the street drew the eyes of everyone they passed. Well, mostly the centre. Jerry and

Archie vied for the lead, straining the engines of their scooters to the max. The engines whined under the strain.

The golf cart had good acceleration, but its top speed just wasn't up to the challenge. That and Norris kept forgetting to keep the accelerator down as he tried to explain to Sky the best way to manage the cart. Despite the fact that he had never driven one before.

Ernie stayed behind them, deciding it was probably safer. He did not want to get struck by an accidental acceleration, or side swiped by a badly timed swerve. The little scooter kept pace with the others with surprising ease, and a fraction of the noise.

'Afternoon.' An elderly woman called out as she passed them on her push bike. There was a moment of silence as she overtook the rest of them, peddling gently. Smiling politely. Expending next to no energy.

All three engines screamed as they tried to accelerate to match the woman's speed. Ernie glanced at Sky. There were no signs of magic in the air, but the old woman was pulling ahead of them a little too quickly.

'Could have beat her on the downhill,' Archie shouted, ignoring the fact she was already so far ahead of them she was a smear on the horizon.

'I could have kept up if not for sticking with you,' Norris shouted back from the golf cart, making Sky wince at the volume.

'Morning.' A young man jogged past them.

Archie yelped, jumping in surprise, and swerving in the runner's direction. Sky's hands twitched towards him, and the scooter swerved back on course.

Ernie scowled at her as the magic dropped away behind them, lowering his own hand and letting go of the magic he had summoned. He could have dealt with it just fine without her.

'Sorry,' Archie shouted. The man looked over his shoulder with a frown, then slowed to a walk, still managing to stay ahead of them.

The engines screamed louder as they tried again to force the scooters past what they were capable of.

'Sky,' Ernie warned quietly as the man started running again. He could feel her smiling. There was no sense of magic, but there was no way that was normal.

The golf cart's engine made a popping sound. Then it sputtered. Smoke belched out the engine, and it ground to a full stop.

'Oh dear,' Sky said, half looking over her shoulder at Ernie. She smiled at him. 'Looks like the engine is having problems.'

'I think it's a sign for us to turn around,' Ernie said, stopping his scooter beside them. Sky just smiled.

'You need a hand?' Archie called out to Norris.

'No, I can fix it. It's just that thing, with the doda on it. You know which one I mean. I don't need any help fixing it,' Norris said, scrambling out of the cab of the Golf car, wafting away some smoke.

'The doda?' Archie said. A grin split his face as he leaned forward on the scooter. 'That next to the dohicky?'

'Fu—'

A horn blared behind them a half second before a car screamed past at a hundred miles an hour, drowning out Norris' voice.

'Watch where you're going, you idiot. Who taught you how to drive?' Norris shouted at the car's fading taillights.

Ernie powered closer to the cart, stopping as he drew level with Sky. 'What did you do?' he asked her quietly as Norris lifted the lid on the engine, muttering under his breath.

'What makes you think I did anything?' Sky said, raising one eyebrow, a smile trying to break through. 'The workings of a vehicle are far too complex for the likes of me.'

'It's steam. It's not important,' Norris shouted to the others.

'Does it have water, then?' Jerry got down off his seat, moving closer to the crowd around Norris. Archie nudged his scooter as close as he could, almost hitting Jerry.

'Complex huh?' Ernie grunted.

'It doesn't need water.' Norris scowled at the others. 'I don't need help.'

'It must have water. How else is it making steam?'

'It's smoke,' Archie said, shaking his head.

'Steam—'

'Do you need a hand, gentlemen?' A man in his twenties had pulled in behind them. 'I've fixed a few cars in my time.'

'Your time?' Archie looked the man up and down as Norris smashed his head on the lid of the engine compartment. Jerry stepped back to watch him mutter. 'You don't have enough age to have done much of anything in your time.'

'I don't need any help. It's a simple fix. Basic really. I just need to do the thingamajig to the whatdoyacallit.'

The man smiled, ducking his head as he tried to hide it.

'Please fix it, before Norris breaks it worse,' Archie said, staring at Norris until his objections puttered off into muttering. 'We don't have all day.'

'Convenient,' Ernie said quietly, watching Sky. 'We are not part of one of your hunts.'

Sky leaned closer until she was level with his ear, then whispered. 'You said it wasn't a hunt.'

'All sorted, it was just loose and needed a refill. You should be good now,' the man said, closing the engine lid, stopping Ernie from responding.

Norris scowled and stomped back to the driver's seat.

'You got a name, boy?' Archie shouted as the man turned to go.

'Charles.' He nodded at them, wiping his hands on his jeans, then offered it to Archie.

'Archie.' They shook, exchanging a quick grin as they both looked sideways at Norris. 'Thanks.'

'Not a problem. Safe journey,' the man said as he hopped into his car and drove off.

'We should head back before something else breaks,' Ernie said, trying again, but Sky ignored him.

'Shall we continue, Gentlemen?' Sky said, smiling as she faced Ernie's glare. 'You are welcome to return, Ernie. We can tell you all about it when we get back.'

There was a chorus of ayes, and the engines started up their high-pitched whine again. There was no way Ernie was going to leave Sky alone. She was up to something; he knew it down to the soles of his shoes. But he was damned if he could see what it was. Until he figured it out, he was not leaving her alone with his people.

WITH ALL THE GOLFCARTS working and back on the road, they regained their previous speed. Or just short of it, at least. Norris gingerly accelerated with more than one glance over his shoulder.

'Where are we going again?' Norris shouted.

Sky winced as he leaned into her ear first. Ernie grinned at her, saying nothing. She wanted to bring them along, she could suffer them for a change.

'To the grandsons,' Jerry said, always with the helpful answers.

'Fu—'

A large motorbike shot past fast enough that it blew up a cloud of dust around them. The three old men coughed like they were trying to hack up their lungs. Ernie coughed twice, loudly. Sky turned to glare at him, brushing dust from her arm.

'What road were we headed to?' Norris asked, trying again with a watery eyed warning glance at Jerry, like he was daring him to say something about it.

'Yule street,' Archie said, spitting out the side of the cart. 'His grandson took over the house a few years ago. Greedy like his grandfather.'

'Yule,' Ernie repeated, sighing. Of course, that's where they were headed.

'Don't worry, Archie. We will get your stuff back,' Sky said, sending a smile over her shoulder.

The road ahead was in a busier part of town, and cars were becoming more frequent. Each one that overtook them passed in an overly wide arc. Of course, there was little choice but to go wide since, between Norris and the rest of them, they took up an entire lane.

'Yule street is this way,' Norris shouted, nodding towards a narrow lane. 'It's a shortcut.'

'For what? A toddler?' Archie said, frowning at the mostly dirt trail.

Ernie suspected a car would barely have made it down the single-track alley. The four of them would probably fit if they could drive in a straight line. One after another. None of which Ernie suspected they would do.

'I've been up here a dozen times before,' Norris said, veering the cart in that direction. 'It's an excellent shortcut.'

The cart teetered at the sharp swerve, making Sky squeak and grab the sidebar. But it didn't get far as they hit the curb. Metal squealed loudly as the cart jerked to a stop, almost unseating Sky and Norris.

Jerry and Archie calmly continued past the crippled cart to the lowered pedestrian crossing a few meters away, then circled back to park in front of the cart on the pavement. Sky sent Ernie a single warning glance, daring him to comment as she straightened in her seat.

'Shortcut?' Archie asked, raising his eyebrow. Norris spluttered.

'I think it might be a good time to call it quits,' Ernie said, watching Sky. She had to be done after this. The cart was not going anywhere.

'You might be right. I think the cart is stuck,' Archie said, half glancing at Ernie, but he couldn't hold back the grin. They might not have been getting close to his justice, but it was good to see the man smiling again. 'You need a hand with that shortcut, Norris?'

'Fu—'

A lorry blasted its horn, the sound vibrating through them as it rumbled past. This time, they all stopped to stare at it, frowning. The man in the front waved at them as if in apology.

'Don't look at me,' Sky said in a low voice that only Ernie could hear. 'Sometimes it's just random.'

Ernie snorted; the timing seemed unlikely.

Norris got out of the cart, shuffling round it, checking it. 'I can fix it.'

The metal was wedged on the curb and the frame looked like it might be bent, or at least twisted.

'I don't—' Archie started.

'I can fix it,' Norris said, narrowing his eyes at them, daring them to argue with him.

'It just needs lifting free, I think. I can give you a hand if you like?' Everyone turned to stare at Charles, who stood in front of his car, now going the opposite way from earlier.

'Please. That would be very kind of you,' Archie said, before Norris could start in again. 'Norris would love the help.'

Sky got down from the cart, moving with delicate grace despite the angle. Ernie stared at the man a little harder, suspicions rising.

'Who is he?' Ernie asked. He could tell by her smile that Sky knew, but she wasn't giving it up that easily.

'Someone who likes to help strangers.' Sky didn't look at Ernie as she spoke. All her focus was on the man. 'Is that so hard to believe?'

Without seeming to extend much in the way of effort, Charles lifted the cart and pushed it back onto the road until all four wheels were even. Surprisingly, they were straight. More surprisingly, there was no other damage.

'Looks like it's all good.' Charles stepped back from his inspection, nodding at Archie before saying goodbye.

'I could have easily fixed it,' Norris said, standing with his arms crossed as Charles drove away. 'Didn't need him.'

'As easy as a shortcut?' Archie asked, raising an eyebrow, on the verge of a smile.

Norris looked both ways with narrowed eyes, then opened his mouth with great venom. 'Fu—'

A fighter jet flew low overhead, whizzing past with two companions on its tail. The noise drowned out everything. Ringing silence followed it as Norris got into the golf cart and slumped like a sulky child.

'Shall we go?' Archie said, struggling to breathe through his laughter.

Sky ducked her head as she got in the golf cart, hiding her own smile. Norris accelerated off without waiting for anyone else. Ernie followed with the others at a more sedate pace.

THE SCOOTERS ONCE AGAIN buzzed down the street, managing a few near misses, some perilous crossings and one stand-off with a grandma at a zebra crossing, before they finally pulled up outside the house of the grandson who'd scammed Archie. As everyone gathered, the amusement that had been present throughout the journey dissipated.

The house was standard picket fence territory. White wood surrounded a two-story detached house with a garage and large garden space. A dog squealed and children yipped. Or possibly the other way around. Either way, it was alive with energy and motion.

'Is this it?' Jerry said, scratching his bald head, eyes on the building. After everything that had led them here, it was obvious they were disappointed.

'It feels like home,' Sky said, glancing at Ernie. 'Love has thrived here, for generation after generation. It's embedded into the foundations of the place, a lifetime of joy.'

The others made noncommittal sounds, but Ernie could feel what she meant. It was rare enough in the modern world to find it, and too easy to lose or destroy. It tingled across his skin, a warm presence that announced itself as 'home'.

'His family has owned this place for longer than anyone could remember. I played here as a boy. This was where the collection started.' Archie's voice was quiet and strained. The pain on his face was like an open wound, raw.

Ernie had memories like those. Bitter and painful when the loss was fresh. Over time, the pain faded until the joy of those moments was all that was left. Ernie hoped Archie could find that happiness again in his memories of his friend. Ernie did not like seeing this pain.

Sky stepped down from the cart to put her hand on Archie's shoulder, offering comfort without words.

Archie sighed. 'We found the first coin buried in this garden.'

'Come on, before we freeze,' Norris said, slipping out of the golf cart with a grunt. The wind that had not bothered them the whole journey picked up. Like a reminder to keep moving forward. 'Let's sucker punch this idiot and get your collection back.'

The abrupt words shook the mood of the group, and Archie hummed his scooter closer, then pulled out a long cane that was tucked into the back. He thumped the door hard with one end.

'Subtle,' Jerry said, grinning as Archie glared at him.

There was a general sound of a war beginning on the other side of the door. After a moment, it opened, and a child who couldn't have been more than five poked her head out. She stared at them with her thumb in her mouth and a toy in the other hand.

'Wodoyouwant?' The garbled words that came from around the thumb made everyone hesitate, exchanging glances.

'Hello little one. We are looking for a gentleman,' Archie said, looking for help. Everyone seemed a little further back, though Ernie hadn't seen anyone move.

'No gentle…' the little girl broke off, giggling, '…men.'

'Maybe your father?'

The little girl stared at him with large eyes and pulled her thumb out of her mouth. 'You're old.'

'Old enough to know what happens to little girls who suck their thumbs,' Archie said, then leaned forward conspiratorially. 'The tooth fairy thinks the thumb is a tooth and takes it with your baby teeth.'

'That's what my grandpap said.' The voice quavered, tears brimming, as she stared at her thumb. Then she showed it to Archie like it was evidence. 'He promised to keep it safe for me.'

Norris sniffed, looking away from them. He was not the only one, as the air grew heavy with shared pain. Loss. The words were so sincere that it made Ernie's throat tight.

'Oh, child,' Archie said, turning so both his feet were on the ground, and he could reach and fold the slimy thumb over her other fingers. 'Your grandpap still does. He thinks you will need it someday.'

Archie spoke with so much sincerity that the little girl looked down at her feet, suddenly shy.

'Sweety, what are you doing?' the man's voice came only a moment before the door was opened wide, revealing a now familiar face. Charles looked at them all one by one until he settled on Archie.

'Grandpap is still keeping my thumb safe, daddy,' the little girl said, then put it back in her mouth.

Charles smiled at the girl, his eyes shining as he patted her on the head. She smiled, then turned and went inside. A few children shouted, some game continuing now the girl had re-joined them.

Ernie was exhausted just watching them. He sent Sky a look, but she ignored him. At least he now had his answer about who Charles was.

'Sorry about that,' Charles said, stepping outside, pulling the door shut behind him. 'They are a bit wild today. Too many kids in one place.'

Archie stared at Charles, the silence dragging on before he finally spoke in a tight voice. 'You look so much like him. I should've seen it sooner.'

'He spoke about you all the time. You're exactly how he described.' Charles smiled.

'You knew who we were when you stopped?' Norris said, narrowing his eyes.

'Who else but Archie would lead an expedition through town in the middle of winter on scooters?' Charles said, raising an eyebrow at Archie like they were sharing an inside joke.

'I miss him,' Archie said, a measure of less pain than there had been.

'Hang on, one sec,' Charles said, darting inside the house with the speed of youth.

'You sure told him,' Norris said, heaving a sigh where he had moved to lean on the golf cart. Archie scowled at him.

Sky sent Ernie a wink as they waited, but Charles was barely gone for a minute before he re-appeared at the door, an old wooden box in his hand. He handed it gently to Archie, helping him settle the weight onto his lap. 'I'm sorry I couldn't bring them sooner. They were locked up in the will.'

'This is—' Archie cut off, voice tight, hand shaking.

'He wanted you to have them, but you know what he was like. Never had time for the legal stuff, and he had never got it written down officially.' Charles crouched, so he was eye to eye with Archie, placing one hand over his. 'I remember the stories he told about how you found each one. He was so proud of the work you put into collecting them.'

Archie opened the box, revealing an unorganised collection of trinkets and coins and other unrecognisable things.

Some were new, others old enough that they looked like little more than scrap metal.

'Would you like to come in? My wife's cooking lunch. I'm sure we can make room for a few more?' Charles asked them. Sincere and honest. The house practically vibrated with pleasure.

'Food? Hell yes,' Norris said, shuffling forward, rubbing his belly like he had been worried it might have disappeared on him. Jerry smiled apologetically, but he followed Norris as they entered the house.

In short order, Charles was helping Archie inside. Another two children of varying ages hovered nearby, asking questions. The feeling of home soaked into them, turning the time of grief into a time of memory and joy.

Ernie waited until they had all gone inside before he turned to Sky. She had shed the modern clothes she'd been wearing, now standing taller by a foot, dressed in old worn leather and fur. 'Why are you here?'

'Do I need a reason?'

'Skadi.' Ernie used her full name, trying to put a growl behind it, but the joy from the house absorbed it. He shook his head at her. 'This was not a hunt.'

'I told you it wasn't, Fryer.' She put emphasis on his own true name. 'You are not the only one who is allowed to take a break and relax in the company of mortals.'

'Who are they to you?' Ernie turned back to the house.

'No one who remembers,' Skadi said. 'No one who will matter in what comes next.'

She put too much emphasis on it. 'My sister sent you then?'

Skadi laughed. 'No one sends me anywhere, Fryer. I am of winter and the hunt. I am free to roam as I choose. Unbound.'

'But?'

'But you can't avoid the future forever. It comes whether you want it to or not,' Skadi said. There was no malice behind it, but it didn't make the words any less true.

'I've time yet.' He turned away as he spoke.

Skadi leaned down to place a light kiss on his cheek, then whispered. 'Not much time.'

When he turned back, she was gone.

Lunch turned out to be a banquet fit for a king, and food enough to fill even Norris. Stories were exchanged around a real fire in a tribute to the dead that Ernie had not seen in a long time.

'It was the strangest thing,' Norris said, scratching at his belly that was bulging even further than normal. 'Happened every time.'

'You imagined it,' Archie said, leaning back in the large armchair he had been helped into like he never planned on leaving.

'Let's experiment, then. Fu—'

'What's exp'iment mean?' the little girl asked, thumb in her mouth. She stared at Norris, waiting.

'Never mind,' Norris said, scowl warring with a smile as he started explaining new words to the child.

All For One

Author's Notes

Those of you who have used hearing aids will know that background noise can be hell, making it hard to follow a conversation. Large gatherings, like family getting together, would mean that there are so many voices that the hearing aids can't keep up. Add that to the way hearing aids eat batteries and you get a very unreliable tool.

So, my grandad's solution would be to turn them off, or down, and then make a best guess at what you had said.

My grandad wasn't a good guesser.

But he was always more than happy to defend—extensively—his best guess about what the conversation had been about.

I sometimes miss trying to put together our conversation, like a puzzle with only half the pieces. I loved being able to bring Albert into this story and bring that slice of my granddad alive with him.

ALL FOR ONE

'You're a thief!'

There was a moment of silence as the words hung heavy in the air.

'Wrong,' Ernie said, making sure his voice was calm, despite the rage that curled inside his stomach. He kept still, reminding himself he was old, slow, and had limited mobility. To do otherwise would lead to questions he didn't want to answer. He liked living at Gard Village—Senior Living retirement home. It was normally quiet.

'You stole Jerry's guitar. I saw you in the corridor,' Vera said, her too wide mouth twisting in a snarl. She hunched over her walking frame to glare at him. The woman was, without a doubt, one of the ugliest people Ernie had seen—and he had seen things no human could even imagine. At seventy, she looked closer to a hundred, but it wasn't the age that had turned her into a gnarled, hunched maggot. No, that was all her personality.

The crowd that had gathered around Vera in the communal living room was small. They shuffled nervously. To be fair, they did everything with a shuffle; at eighty and over, they were not as mobile as they had once been. The nervous energy was new. But then Vera knew how to wear people down, and she'd only been there a week.

Ernie could have walked away then—he hadn't stolen it. But he couldn't just let it go. A challenge had been issued.

'I did not steal from anyone here,' Ernie said, letting his voice carry.

The silence that greeted his words grated on him. Each eye flicked nervously to Vera as no one said anything.

'Of course not.' A single woman's voice from the back of the group spoke up. The crowd parted for her, happy to let her take the brunt of Vera's gaze. Betty was a thin and delicate woman that always reminded Ernie of a doll. Her hair was thick with lush silvery curls, despite her age. 'Ernie is no thief.'

'I saw—'

'You saw wrong. I'd bet my winning hand on it.' Betty's chin lifted, until she was staring down her nose at Vera. 'Jerry has not even said his guitar is missing, and even if it was, he is lucky to remember where he left it half the time.'

Vera clicked forward on her walking frame. 'Are you such a coward, Ernie, that you let a woman fight your battles?'

Ernie barked a laugh. It brought Vera's scowl back to him. Or maybe that was just her normal expression. 'Betty is more than capable of being my champion. If I needed one.'

Betty beamed at him, and the mood of the crowd shifted. An almost visible wave of pleasure and joy. No one liked Vera. Seeing her put in her place was a far more entertaining game. They dispersed in relative quiet.

Vera watched them go, anger still twisting her face. 'Do you think they will stand by you for long when they find out what you really are?' She turned and stalked away before he could reply. Her walker thumping on the ground heavily.

Ernie let her go without comment, but his gut still churned with anger and the unwanted certainty that Vera was far from done.

IT TOOK ERNIE A few hours to cool his anger to a simmer. He sat in a chair at the edge of the communal living room, deliberately ignoring everyone. At least until Betty entered with a face like a thundercloud. As she focused on Ernie, he knew he was in trouble.

'Ernie Smith.' Betty's voice was cold. 'A word.'

As Ernie got up to follow Betty, he glimpsed Vera at the second door. She sent him a slow smile that made her look like a snake, cold and poisonous. He didn't have to think hard about what had upset Betty.

'You told someone,' Betty gritted out between clenched teeth, barely waiting for him to join her in the hallway. She started walking in a fast shuffle almost immediately, not stopping until they were outside of the hearing range of anyone in the room. Which wasn't far.

'You need to give me more than that,' Ernie said, grunting as she sent him another glare. This was not going well.

'You told them about my wig. They know.' Betty spat the second word, curling her lip like it left a foul taste in her mouth.

'I did not tell them,' Ernie said, grabbing Betty's arm as she started to turn away. Anger rose again. He pushed it down. He was not the only one who had been wronged here. Betty's hair was a source of pride for her. Fake or not, it did not matter to him. But it did to her.

'They know. They are laughing at me, Ernie. Me!' Betty swung from angry to tears. Her pain was a harsh stain on the air around him.

'It wasn't me.' Ernie softened his voice as he spoke. 'I told no one.'

Betty shook her head, touching her hair that had swung forward. 'If it wasn't you, then who?'

'You don't believe I was a thief, but you believe I would give out secrets?' Ernie asked, his own anger rising.

She turned away, shrugging out of his grip. When she spoke, he couldn't see her face. 'No one else knew. Except you.' She shook her head, then walked away from him.

He let her go. There was nothing he could say that would convince her.

'Another person betrayed. I don't know why they put up with you, Ernie. You hardly seem worth their while,' Vera said from behind him.

Ernie walked away before he said or did something he would regret later. He reminded himself that the woman was only human. As angry as he was, she did not deserve what he could hit her with.

But human or not, he needed to get rid of Vera before she poisoned the whole place. This was his home, and he was damned if he was just going to give it to her.

Ernie stalked outside, stopping to take a slow breath to calm down. The reaction of the other residents had not hit him as hard as Betty's doubt had. That she would believe this lie made his chest ache.

Two residents stood at the corner of the building like teenagers sneaking cigarettes at school, drawing deeply and spluttering almost as much. They eyed Ernie suspiciously. He tried to ignore them.

There had been more than one occasion in his life where he had wished to be left alone. Now that he had it, it felt wrong.

He had to find a way to get rid of Vera. No one seemed to like the woman, but it wasn't stopping them from listening. The longer she was here, the worse it got.

He considered using her tricks against her. A thief is not welcome. But she wasn't trying to be welcomed, she was trying to batter everyone into her way of thinking. To turn them against Ernie and make them paranoid. He had to find a different way to get rid of her.

Two familiar men appeared in the doorway. They both paused to frown suspiciously at the two smokers on the corner, then headed for Ernie.

'Don't let Vera win, Ernie. No one believes her,' Jerry said. He was a squat man in his eighties with almost no hair, and a frown so heavy that it half covered his eyes. 'I know you didn't steal my guitar.'

Abraham stood behind Jerry, nodding in agreement. He was a wispy man that had once been a lot heavier, and his warped frame showed the strain of that weight. 'Yes. You should get that checked. That kind of thing can spread,' Abraham said confidently.

There was a moment of hesitation while they replayed the conversation in their heads. Completely failing to find any possible way to make Abraham's words fit. His hearing had been going for as long as Ernie had known him. Now that he was sitting just the other side of ninety, it had almost abandoned him altogether.

'Turn your hearing aid on,' Jerry shouted in Abraham's ear.

'No need to yell,' Abraham shouted, almost as loud as he leaned away from Jerry. He did touch his hearing aid, though Ernie could have sworn it looked like he turned it down, not on.

Jerry rolled his eyes and turned back to Ernie. 'No one believes her.'

Behind them, the retirement home's only couple stepped outside, eyeing the two men smoking, then tightened their grips on each other and turned and walked the other way. The suspicion and doubt were almost a visible wave between them.

'Not everyone agrees with you,' Ernie said, shaking his head.

'I'm here if you need to talk,' Jerry said, slapping Ernie's shoulder as he turned with Abraham and shuffled back inside.

As the couple turned the corner of the building, Ernie realised they hadn't even looked at him. But they were still huddling together, like they were afraid. Now he thought about it. The two smokers were far enough away that even with their glasses, they wouldn't have recognised Ernie either.

This wasn't just about Vera's accusation against Ernie anymore. The suspicion and doubt were spreading like a virus through his home. Was this more than just Vera poisoning them against Ernie?

Ernie cursed. The ground under his feet smouldered as his rage peaked. He stepped on it hurriedly, hoping no one would notice the singed flowers. It was a wasted use of energy; it wasn't like he could use magic against Vera. That would be like swatting a fly with a building.

But something felt wrong, almost unnatural in the way the suspicion was spreading. But he'd sensed nothing out of place and if something external was affecting people, he should have. Or at least he thought he would have.

He had been here a lot of years, all the time pretending to be human. Had he let his senses fade, forgotten the basics?

He turned back towards the building, his home. Maybe it was time to dust off that part of himself that he had been ignoring.

ERNIE ROLLED HIS SHOULDERS as he blew off the layers of dust from his little used senses. These were more than just the physical sense of touch or sight. It was more ephemeral, and something few humans had, and fewer still came close to understanding.

He let the extra sense spread out from him in a wide arc, like a blanket gently covering the retirement home. Or that's how he tried to do it; it was more a stutter, like a net that kept getting caught on every little outcrop. Tangled and full of holes. Information flowed in an almost overwhelming stream.

Despite the overload of his senses, he could feel the taint on everything. It wasn't exactly magic, but nor was it natural. Like an oil stain after a car accident, a consequence of something else.

He almost missed the magic underneath. A subtle silky web against his coarse net. If he hadn't opened himself up, he would never have known it was happening. It tingled against his skin, sparking through against the threads of his net. He had been right, something was wrong. He followed subtler magic, stalking through the building, avoiding people as much as he could.

When he came to the end of the trail, he stopped. The door in front of him was closed, and more than just familiar. It led into his own room.

His anger spiked again. He worked to calm it as he shoved the wood harshly, making the figure inside jump and spin to stare at him.

Vera glared as if he was intruding on her personal space, not the other way around.

'What are you doing?' Ernie let the words out slowly.

'Proving you're a liar.' She held onto the old woman act with everything she had, hunched and twisted as she stood in the middle of his room. But she was missing something.

'Without your walker?' Ernie asked, walking around the room slowly, tapping the metal frame as he moved past it. Vera twitched, but it was already too late to bluff, even without the feel of magic still in the air. Whatever it had been was falling apart like a tapestry being unwoven. 'You're proving someone is a liar. Who are you?'

Magic tinged the air again, no longer hidden, and Vera's image wavered until a tall brunette stood in front of him. She had tanned skin and chocolate eyes that matched her hair. This close, the magic was familiar, even if the form had not been.

'Verthandi.' Ernie all but growled her name. The recognition was not a welcome one. 'Why are you here?'

'Not everything is about you, Ernie,' Verthandi said, twisting his name as she spoke, like it left a bad taste in her mouth. Interesting that she hadn't used his true name when he'd used her's.

'I don't see anyone else that you are irritating. It's not a hard conclusion to come to. Call me Sherlock and leave.'

'You think it's that easy?' Her voice was heavy with venom. 'I'm not done yet.'

'Then answer the question. Why are you here?'

'Why not?' she said, mouth twisting into a smile.

'There is nothing here for you. You're not invited.' Ernie stressed the word invited, but it only made her smile widen.

'I like it here. It's a public home, open to anyone who wants to pay to live here,' Vera said. The old woman's visage settled over her again as she stalked past him and roughly grabbed the walking frame. 'Everyone is so accommodating.'

'You're not welcome here,' Ernie said through gritted teeth.

'Then make me leave?' Vera smiled, showing teeth. 'Of course, then there wouldn't be much left for you to live in. Choices, choices.'

Before Ernie could reply, a nurse poked her head around his door, forcing a smile at them as she feigned interest. 'Everything all right in here?'

'No problem.' Vera nodded, clomping forward with the walker. Before she left, she whispered just loud enough for him to hear. 'I think I will stay a while longer.'

Ernie didn't try to stop her; there was little point. She was right. He didn't want to get into an all-out magic fight with her; they would destroy more than just this one building. And to try human level force to throw her bodily out would have just meant the staff would toss him out behind her.

She had made it clear she wasn't going to leave of her own free will.

He only had one choice now. If she would not leave on her own, he had to find someone who she would listen to. He had to go see her sisters.

ERNIE STOPPED AT THE roots of the giant world tree until it came into proper focus. The layers of the world were heavy here, overlapping uncomfortably like a sponge being squeezed to half its size. Just because it could be squished that way didn't mean it felt good.

The house he was looking for was in one of the deeper layers. The forest expanded around him—pines, oaks, and yews all mixed with other trees that humans had no name for. Some had been long gone from the world for centuries. The branches created a canopy of shade so thick that even the rain wouldn't make it through. In the centre of it all, was a cottage made from logs and thatch. It felt out of place compared to where he had been living. This home had no place in the modern world.

Ernie took a step forward, the distance twisting around him until he was standing on the doorstep. He knocked on the door; the sound echoed in the room beyond. The wind blew chimes that had been set in the nearby trees.

'You weren't invited,' a woman's voice said from behind the door.

'Looks like we have something in common. I didn't invite your sister to my home,' Ernie said, letting the anger settle into his voice.

The door opened slowly, revealing a young woman in a plain brown dress that looked homemade. Milky white skin and hair so blond it could have been spun gold. Her eyes mirrored the colour, a golden shade that no human would ever have.

'What did she do now?' Urth asked, crossing her arms, narrowing her eyes at him like it was his fault.

'She has moved in without my permission.'

'You live in an open home for abandoned humans.' Another voice spoke from behind him. He didn't turn to look at Skuld.

She moved around him to stand next to her sister. You would never have guessed they were related. Where her sister was light, she was dark. Her skin was a rich mahogany, and her hair the colour of autumn leaves. Much like her sister, her eyes were the same mirrored hue as her hair. Another colour humans would never have.

'They are not abandoned,' Ernie said, though the reality was a partial truth. But it sounded far too much like she was comparing them to an animal rescue centre, not a retirement home. 'It doesn't make it any less my home.'

Skuld curled a lock of red hair around her finger. 'If you don't find her company acceptable, then leave.' She paused, then smiled slowly. 'I've seen how it ends.'

She wasn't being figurative. Skuld had the ability to see what had yet to come. But like most things relating to the future, that view was more like watching a ship travel the rough ocean waves. The path was not easy to predict.

'Skuld,' Urth said, a warning clear in her voice. She was always the calmer of the three, she saw the past, and the burden of being able to see so much more than any one person should. She turned to him. 'What Verthandi does is not within our control. She'll come back when she is ready.'

Which meant they had fallen out again. Vera was all about the present. The moment. Why she had decided that in this moment she wanted to ruin Ernie's retirement, he did not know. If her sisters did, they were not giving him any help.

The three women together were the Norn's of destiny. They could be dangerous when they were agreeable-which was not often, thankfully. But when they were fighting, it was a whole other kind of problem.

'One, or both of you, know why she has decided to invade my home,' Ernie said, narrowing his eyes at the two of them. They exchanged glances. Something unspoken passed between them. Energy crackled. 'I want her gone.'

'No,' Skuld said.

'If you think she will bully me out of my life, you're sorely mistaken.'

'Without using any of your power?' Urth asked. Ernie's eye twitched. He had hoped they would not pick up on that part. 'I thought so. The choice is yours, of course. If you wish to use power to remove her, you are welcome to try.'

'What happened?' Ernie tried again.

'She is sulking, like she always does. She will get bored.' Skuld's voice was cold, uncaring. But there was an under-current he couldn't read.

'Enough. You have your answer,' Urth said sharply, glaring at Skuld. Again, something unspoken passed between them.

Ernie spun and walked away, frustrated. This had got him nothing but a headache from the weight of the layers of time pressing on him. His ears popped as he passed outside their effect. He had to find another way to get rid of Vera.

Though he was starting to understand why she did not want to go home if this was how they were treating her. He needed to find out what Vera wanted. How hard could that be?

As SOON AS HE got home, Ernie knew something was off. He followed the sound of voices down the hallway. Half a dozen familiar faces stood outside the door to his room.

'He is lying to you,' Vera yelled, almost into Abraham's ear.

'My dear, I'm flattered, really. But my wife would disapprove,' Abraham shouted. Shaking his head as if he were disappointed in the woman.

'Lying. Lying.' Vera tried again, stretching out the words like she thought that would help.

'Now, now, miss. There is no need for that kind of language.' Abraham stepped back from her.

Vera gave him a disgusted look and turned to the small group of other residents instead.

'All we need to do is check his room,' Vera said, hand resting on the door handle. She saw him at the back of the crowd, eyes narrowed as she shoved the door open.

She thumped the walker inside. The small group, that included Betty and Jerry, followed her into Ernie's room. His space. Small though it was, it was his.

'This is not appropriate, Vera,' Betty said. Despite her words, she took the room in with a slow glance, curiosity, and interest, not suspicion. He felt a little like she had stripped him down to his underwear. 'This isn't your r oom.'

'You wanted proof? Here is your proof,' Vera said. The reason she had been in his room crystallised a moment before she opened the door to his closet.

Jerry's guitar stood out amongst his clothes. Black polished wood, with gold metal work all over it. Its distinctive design was a familiar sight around the building, even though Jerry's hands were so gnarled he could hardly play now.

Ernie met Vera's eyes; his anger barely contained. She'd put it in his room. Just to do this. He spun on his heel and walked away. A few voices shouted after him, but he ignored them.

THE LOOK ON THE faces of the other residents, his friends, irritated Ernie. It was like a TV show on repeat. They had believed Vera. The so-called proof was enough for them.

In the hour he had walked, he had circled around the problem in so many ways that there was really only one answer he could come up with. He didn't want to be somewhere that people did not trust him.

He was no longer angry. He was done.

The hallways were empty when he came back to his room. No one was about, which suited him fine.

He opened his door and froze. There was a crowd of people there.

Jerry jumped, his hand going to his heart as he glared at Ernie. There were others there too, each one of them grinning. Betty turned, smiling at Ernie as she elbowed Abraham.

'What?' Abraham said, rubbing the spot on his chest where the elbow had struck. 'We tied her up. What more do you want?'

'Ernie is back,' Betty said. But not loud enough.

'I know we have to wait until Ernie is back,' Abraham said. Grunting. He turned then, blinked rapidly, then nudged Betty. 'Why didn't you tell me he was here?'

Betty rolled her eyes and tugged at his sleeve to pull him aside. Behind them sat Vera. She was bound and gagged on the floor at the end of his bed. She glared at him. With the humans so close, she couldn't use her magic without risking being outed.

'I know it's not your birthday. But we have a present for you,' Betty said. Her smile turned wicked. 'I'm sorry I said those things earlier, but I had to make her believe me.'

Vera struggled against the thick rope weakly, motions stilted as she held to her image. Ernie did not ask where the rope had come from. There were answers he did not need. Ever.

'Knew it wasn't you, mate,' Jerry said, slapping Ernie's shoulder. 'Leaves only one person.'

Ernie blinked rapidly as something flew in his eye.

ERNIE CONVINCED THEM TO untie Vera. They did it reluctantly, then they filed out of his room, already talking about setting up a poker game. Jerry was the last to leave, blinking in confusion as he looked around Ernie's room. He gave Vera a blank look, then left. Vera was already fading from their minds as whatever spell she had been weaving lost its hold, and it was taking the memories with it

.

'Are you going to leave on your own?' Ernie asked as he walked beside her towards the exit. She had abandoned her walker now, walking straight-backed, with her chin high.

'It's obvious I'm not welcome anymore,' Vera said, not looking at him as they hit the front door. He didn't add that she had never been welcome. It seemed unnecessarily harsh.

'Why do this?' Ernie said as she started to walk away.

She stopped, looking over her shoulder at him. 'I want what you have here.'

'You were envious?' Ernie squashed the laugh that rose in his chest. Considering he had won; it was in bad taste. 'I live in a hole for the forgotten.'

'Forgotten by who?' Vera said, turning all the way back to him.

Ernie shook his head. 'Their families have moved on. Chosen to let them go already because it might hurt less that way. They are forgotten, abandoned like your sister said.'

'That is not forgotten.' She looked down at her hands, shaking her head. 'I always live in the present. Always. No one remembers me for long. I am a fleeting moment in the lives of others. I wanted to be remembered. Like they remember you. Like their family remembers them.'

'There are better ways to be remembered,' Ernie said. This time, the snort escaped.

Vera shuddered. 'It's harder for people to forget someone they don't like. But even then, now that the magic is gone, they have forgotten me already.'

He said nothing to that. He hadn't known that was the cost of Vera's gift, though he didn't imagine her sister's abilities came at any lighter price, just a different one. Looking at it from Vera's perspective, he could see what she meant. Abandoned was not forgotten, though it might felt that way at times. Vera was always forgotten.

'I remember you,' he said at last.

'It is not the same, Freyr. They stood together behind you tonight, even though I showed them the guitar. They never believed it could have been you.' She shook her head. The faint echo of power as she used his true name made his skin tingle. 'Is it so bad to want that?'

'You could have chosen to live anywhere,' Ernie said. 'Why try to take what I had?'

'You're going to be leaving soon, anyway. Skuld said it's coming.' Vera shivered.

'But it's not here yet,' Ernie said as he rested his hand on her shoulder with a sigh.

He hesitated to let her leave when she was in so much pain. The form she had chosen had changed, slipping back into the young woman. How could someone so old look so young and lost? He wanted to do something more for her, despite what she had done. He remembered her sisters. The way they had talked about her.

'Would you like to lose a game of poker?' he asked, surprising himself. Not the losing part. No one won but Betty, but the game could be fun. 'I'll make sure they remember us.' He had the power to give her that, even if it was just a small moment in time.

Vera blinked at him in surprise, then smiled shyly, the pleasure warming her features. 'I'd love that.'

'Next time, just ask,' Ernie said, shaking his head. Though he did hope there wasn't a next time.

118

Grandad Swap

Author's Notes

MY GRANDDAD WAS OLD-FASHIONED in many ways. He hated it when I swore, though he didn't complain often. I remember having more than one conversation with him about it; never a reprimand, but a reminder that he didn't like swearing around women. That belief went both ways. He never swore in front of me, either.

There were other places where this odd set of beliefs would come up, usually in an attempt at humour that was not always appropriate. One phrase sticks with me, even years later…'That's not a skirt, that's a belt.' Any skirt that sat at knee level or above was a chance to use the joke.

As I wrote this story, I wanted to include that small piece of him, that joke he loved so much, even if it was a very small part of the character. To all my family who are heaving a sigh at hearing this well-worn joke once again, tough luck.

Remembered and not forgotten.

GRANDAD SWAP

Ernie ducked outside, letting out a relieved breath as he avoided a troupe of toddler wielding visitors.

The seasonal Father's Day rush had brought a wave of guilty children, most clutching babies, flowers, and chocolate like it could shield them from the reality of their own future. As a result, there were too many damn people in too small a space. Escape had seemed like the best option.

Ernie took a slow breath, but only managed to choke in more smoke than air. Irritated, he turned to find the source.

A man leaned against the Gard Village—Senior Living's sign, his back to Ernie, phone pressed against his ear, and a cigarette in his free hand. Between his too-small t-shirt and skin-tight jeans, it was a wonder he could take in any breath at all.

Ernie was at his limit of condescending smiles, and people in general, so he turned, every intention of walking away, but the man's next words stopped him.

'He'll be dead soon. When he's gone, I'll get the lot,' the man said, taking another deep draw from his cigarette, not even looking around to see if someone was there. Like it was not a concern. 'Maybe then you'll be happy?'

Ernie told himself he didn't care; after all, it was none of his business. But he couldn't quite make himself walk away.

It wasn't even like the words were a great surprise. Hell, most of the children were here for the same reasons, even if they were subtler about it. The greed of the young was one of the common reasons that the residents had any visitors at all.

'If I'm not here, how can I convince him that I care?' the man said, brushing a wayward strand of hair back into the nest on his head. It was styled with a messy deliberateness that was not possible without effort. Half a ton of wax, two cans of hairspray and a bottle of industrial glue later, most people would have given up.

'Excuse me,' Ernie said, tapping the man on the shoulder. Anger was a little fire in the pit of his stomach.

The man turned, blowing smoke in Ernie's face, and said, 'Do you mind, old man? I'm having a private conversation.'

Ernie recognised him. Liam came weekly, showing what Ernie now knew was fake kindness to his grandfather, Jerry. Liam had little backbone, less sense, and had so far survived on family money to live a life he had not earned.

Jerry appeared in the doorway before Ernie could respond. Jerry had a permanent scowl that looked to have been ingrained at about age thirty and had simply got deeper as the years wore on.

Liam changed between one blink and the next, plastering a smile across his face, almost dropping his phone, and burning himself with his cigarette in his haste to rush over and greet his grandfather.

'Granddad, it's so good to see you,' Liam said in a 'too loud' voice that all grandchildren used when dealing with those older than them. As if by being old, they somehow lost common sense, hearing, and had forgotten everything that person knew.

Jerry's frown deepened, eyebrows almost folding over his eyes. He glanced between Ernie and Liam, as the latter continued a stream of words, not allowing Ernie a chance to speak.

Liam's voice grated on Ernie's brain, making the little fire of anger burn brighter. He needed to be taught a lesson. Something to make him understand what his grandfather's life was like.

Ernie took a quick look around. No one else was about except the three of them. He let his magic rise, willing it into shape, then clicked his fingers.

The sound echoed unnaturally around him, then wavered halfway between a sound and a pulse of energy, but not by design. Ernie waved his hand at the stalled magic to hurry it along, as it almost forgot why it was there. With a twitch, the pulse hit the two men.

Jerry and his grandson blinked at each other as their souls settled into their new bodies.

ERNIE WATCHED AS JERRY touched his head, faint horror creeping over his expression as his fingers caught and almost stuck to the super glue concoction in his hair. He rolled his eyes upwards, staring at it.

Liam folded in on himself, hand going to his back while simultaneously trying to take the weight off one knee and rub the other. It looked like he was trying to do some kind of acrobatic feat, but in reality, the mix of pain and stiffness was just a normal day for Jerry's body. It was just that Liam's mind had never had to deal with it before.

Jerry, in Liam's body, took a step away from them, eyes flickering between Liam and Ernie.

Liam, who was now touching Jerry's bald head in horror, focused on his own body retreating away from him, eyes widening.

Jerry smiled, turned, and jogged towards Liam's car, hand already fishing in his pocket for the keys.

'Nooo,' Liam cried, trying to give chase. A short shuffle followed, his slipper-covered feet dragging on the pavement as he fought for speed. But he was no longer a slim twenty-year-old. One of the staff, who had wandered out to see what the shouting had been about, spotted his desperate not-dash and intervened.

'Come now, dear,' she said, pivoting Liam's shuffle, so he was heading back into the building.

'He stole my body,' Liam wailed. The woman pursed her lips, rolling her eyes.

Ernie hid his smile as he followed them inside.

'Calm down, Jerry.' There was a quick pat on the arm, and an indulgent smile that people often put on when dealing with those who were old.

'That's not my name. I'm not meant to be here.' Liam pulled out of the woman's grip and tried to grab her. Years of avoiding old men who should have known better had made her agile. Barely looking like she had moved at all, she regained her hold on his arm and continued leading him away.

'Of course you're not, Jerry,' she said, trying to soothe him, waving to another staff member. She disappeared to get the 'for emergencies' pills that were kept just for this very occasion.

The pills disappeared into Liam's mouth as the woman helped him swallow them with a practised ease that Liam didn't know how to deal with. Jerry had been a pro at hiding those he did not want and moving them on in the regular poker game without the staff being any the wiser.

Ernie smiled as he listened to the car rev, gears grinding as Jerry tried to remember how to drive. *Yes,* Ernie thought happily, *that had worked quite well.*

DROOL DRIBBLED DOWN LIAM'S chin as another round of pills kept him just out of reach of the real world.

Two days had passed, and Ernie had expected Jerry to have returned by now, growing bored with the body. He hadn't.

So instead of watching a doomed poker game, Ernie was stuck watching Liam. They were sitting in the outdated communal living room, where the staff could watch the people who needed an extra pair of eyes on them.

'It had been such a good idea,' Ernie said to Liam. Ernie did not add that somehow the amusement had been short-lived; he would not admit he missed Jerry, not even to himself.

Liam ignored him.

Magic stirred like a summer's breeze around Ernie, a familiar forewarning of a visitor he could do without. He did not need this now.

A petite, blond woman walked in, looking no more than twenty in that body. She made no effort to hide or mask her presence and several heads turned towards her. Mostly the old men.

A member of staff moved to intercept her, giving her a harried smile. 'May I help you?'

'Hi, I'm Leigh, I'm here to see my uncle?' Leigh said, pointing towards Ernie. That wasn't her real name, just as Ernie wasn't really her uncle, but it was simpler than her true one. Very few of Ernie's family used their true names.

'Of course, dear, Ernie loves visitors,' the staff said, nodding her head in Ernie's direction like he was a prize on a game show.

Leigh smiled in thanks and took a seat opposite him. 'Uncle Ernie,' she said, rolling the word out longer than was necessary.

'What do you want?' Ernie asked, watching her with narrowed eyes.

'You can't leave them like this,' Leigh said, ignoring his question, giving Liam a rather direct look. Not that Ernie had really expected she would be here about anything else.

'It's under control,' Ernie said, just at the same moment that a small sliver of black joined the clear drool pouring from the corner of Liam's mouth.

'So, you plan on killing them both?' She leaned forward, raising an eyebrow. 'I felt the power you used to do this across town. If you wanted to kill them, there were easier ways.'

'They aren't going to die,' Ernie said, trying not to sound defensive. It was only a tiny bit of black. He reached out and wiped it away, the tissue already dark from the last time he had cleaned Liam's chin. 'I will swap them back once Jerry has had his fun.'

'And if he doesn't come back?' Leigh's echo of his own thoughts made him shiver. 'The others will not be happy with that.'

'I'm retired. What do I care what the others think or do?' Ernie did care, though not for those reasons. Retirement was all about being left alone—except by the guilty family who visited from time to time.

'The humans are going to get very upset when people start bleeding black blood from their eye sockets. That will be noticed,' Leigh said, raising her eyebrow at him. 'Everyone will care about that.'

'What?' Ernie asked, looking at Liam again. More drool dripped from his chin in a long, slippery string. It didn't look that bad.

'Don't you even know what you've done?' Leigh asked. When he didn't answer, she shook her head and pulled a handkerchief from one of her pockets. Her hands moved with the care of a healer as she wiped his chin. 'The souls are rotting. That kind of damage will spread and infect other people.'

'I didn't want that,' Ernie said at last. He remembered the way that magic had stalled out when he had tried to switch the souls. He'd forced the energy forward. That had been stupid, careless. He knew better.

Days like today had him wishing for the excuse of senility that came with actual human age.

'I know you didn't, Ernie,' Leigh said, somehow managing not to sound condescending as she patted his hand. 'But please, fix it. I don't want to deal with a plague.'

Ernie nodded. That hadn't been the plan. It was just supposed to have been a lesson.

She gave him one last look before she stood and left. A few of the feistier old men wolf whistled at her as she passed.

Ernie shoved his chair back and got to his feet. It was time to make Jerry come back.

FINDING JERRY PROVED TO be more difficult than Ernie had first thought. The town was small enough that it only had one strip club, two moderately safe poker clubs, one il-legal-stab-you-in-the-back-alley poker club, and one dance club. It did, of course, have other things as well. But some-how, he suspected that Jerry, in a twenty-five-year-old's body, was not likely to stop by a supermarket. No one went there except when it was time to choose between starving or surviving, and even then, some people really did have to think hard about their options.

The illegal poker club had been a good guess, Ernie reasoned, as he slipped through the gathering crowd. He glanced back at the flames dancing over the building as he neatly tucked his winnings into his jacket. The wrong guess, but a good one.

The illegal poker club's fire had not been his fault. The trail of alcohol leading from the bar to the smokers' garden had been him, of course, but not the fire. Next time they tried to cheat, stab, and bury someone, they would think twice. That was if anything was left of their club after the fire was done.

Ernie had already checked the legal poker clubs to no success. Next up was the strip club, but a squeal made him turn. Half-dressed strippers poured out into the street from the building next door, a wave of water hitting them.

One of the firemen hastily turned back to the fire, taking the hose with him, still sneaking glances over his shoulder at the women.

There was no sign of Jerry among the confused, damp, and angry looking patrons and strippers.

Ernie sighed. That only left the dance club. He shuddered, heading towards it, dragging his feet.

It wasn't really the dance club that was the problem. Not really. It was the noise. The light. The smell. And of course, the people. Far too many people in too small a place. The club itself would have been fine if it had been sanitised and the sticky residue removed.

The people who went to the club disagreed. The dance music all but ran through their blood, and the lights made the strange new dance moves less ridiculous. The smell was like a drug—sweat and stale bodies made the air ripe.

Okay, maybe that was a step too far, Ernie thought. Even they couldn't think it smelled good. But it was what earned the Club its capital C. That and the people who named it had no imagination.

Ernie was already regretting coming at all when he finally spotted Jerry.

He was grinding against a woman who could have been his great-great-granddaughter. She was a tiny mouse of a girl with a skirt so short it might as well have been called a belt.

Ernie pushed through the crowd until he finally stood in front of Jerry.

'Are you real?' Jerry asked, glancing up at Ernie with glassy eyes. Lipstick smeared his cheek and neck.

Jerry had dressed like it was the nineteen fifties. He wore a fedora despite the heat, and a suit jacket open wide, white shirt clinging to his body underneath. He was rather fortunate that the style happened to have rolled round to this decade. The week that followed it would change again, and he may not have fit so well. Another woman danced so close behind that she was all but dry humping him.

Ernie sighed; he was about a whole bottle of whisky too late to get Jerry to listen to reason. Ernie considered leaving him there, but a small trickle of black came out of Jerry's nose. Jerry wiped it away on his sleeve, not even noticing the colour.

'I'm real today,' Ernie said as he reached between the women to grab Jerry's arm.

'What?' Jerry staggered.

'It's time to go home,' Ernie said, dragging Jerry out of the building.

AT THE ENTRANCE TO the retirement home, Jerry seemed to sober up. He pulled free from Ernie's grip, wiping away a thin black line of snot that leaked from his nose. Ernie winced as he saw it, the reminder of the damage he'd caused unwelcome.

'No,' Jerry said, as he swayed and then turned and started to jog across the car park. This time Ernie had the car keys, so there really was no escape. Ernie waited for the inevitable.

Jerry's jog slowed to a walk, then shuffle, then to a dead stop as he bent over double, coughing up lungs that had seen too many cigarettes. The soul rot probably wasn't helping either.

Ernie helped Jerry back to the door, tuning out the faint grumble about things that were not anatomically possible.

Ernie shoved Jerry down in the seat next to his grandson. They blinked at each other. Some of the drugs had worn off, and the grandson was no longer drooling. He alternated between glaring balefully at the young woman who was on duty and staring at Jerry.

The woman scowled at Ernie in disapproval. He ignored her until she stalked away, leaving them alone.

'You don't have to do this,' Jerry said, glancing at Liam, who was glaring at Jerry's clothes.

'If I don't, you will die,' Ernie said. He had no desire to be responsible for that, let alone a plague.

'Death might not be so bad?' Jerry said, not looking at Ernie. Jerry had often spoken of his belief that lives had a limit, an end. He was fairly sure he had missed his exit.

'You will both die,' Ernie said.

Liam spoke at the same time as Ernie. 'You don't get to leave me that easily.'

Jerry and Ernie blinked at Liam in surprise. The grandson grunted, looking away.

Ernie let the silence stand as he pulled the magic together and set to swapping the two men back. When he clicked his fingers to release it, the magic jumped to action, this time moving without hesitation as it covered the two men.

The lines of black that had been starting to drip from Liam's nose faded and disappeared. He stretched his hands as he settled back in his chair, relief on his face.

'I am not sure this is an improvement,' Jerry said, waving his hand through his own head as it slumped forwards towards the table.

Liam jumped to his feet as Jerry collapsed. Ernie was surprised; for the first time, he really did see true concern in the grandson's eyes.

'Am I dead?' Jerry asked mournfully where he stood behind his body, rather than inside it. 'I was hoping for something a little more exciting for my end.'

Ernie resisted the urge to answer Jerry, focusing on the woman who had come to check on them. Having the staff think Ernie was talking to invisible people would not have been helpful.

'This is just sad. Oh. I wonder if...' Jerry trailed off, moving away.

'He's fine,' she said, hand hovering over Jerry, thankfully not checking his pulse. He had spent half the day falling asleep in exactly the same position. She didn't know that he was actually dead at that moment, without his soul, but Ernie was going to fix it. Hopefully, before she figured it out. Going by the way she was smiling at Liam; it was a good bet it could be awhile.

Jerry was already gone by the time Ernie stood, stepping away from the pair. He cursed silently. Jerry wouldn't be able to go far from his body, but in this place, with invisibility and the ability to walk through walls, there really was only one place he would go.

ERNIE THOUGHT IT WAS best to make himself invisible, too. Being found in someone else's bathroom really wasn't something he wanted to explain. From experience, Ernie knew that these things were not acceptable, regardless of age.

Tapping Jerry on the shoulder, Ernie waited for the man to pull his head back from where it was inside the shower wall. 'What are you doing?'

'Are you dead as well?' Jerry asked, giving him an odd look. 'It's probably the pills they have been giving us. Poor quality.'

'No, I'm not dead.' Ernie's eyes lingered on the steam coming out of the shower. The sound of an old Elvis song, words half in tune, echoed out. 'Neither are you. It's time to go back.'

'Five minutes?' Jerry asked, leaning back towards the wall, smiling. His head disappeared before Ernie could answer. The chill of Jerry's presence turned the water so cold that Betty's singing managed to hit a note that was not designed for human hearing.

'Now.' Ernie dragged Jerry back, wincing at the pain in his ears.

'I'm dead. I don't have to go back,' Jerry said, reluctantly letting himself be dragged. 'I don't have to be in pain anymore.'

'It's not your time yet, Jerry,' Ernie said.

'What if I want it to be?' Jerry's voice broke faintly.

Ernie stared at him. He knew he would never feel what Jerry felt, never really grow old like he did, no matter how he pretended.

'All the more reason to fight,' Ernie said, placing a hand on Jerry's shoulder. 'There are people who need you still.'

'Liam doesn't need me. I'm a burden.' Jerry looked away.

'Is that why he comes every week?' Ernie said, stepping closer.

'He wants my money.' Jerry snorted. 'Wants more than he's earned.'

Ernie took Jerry's arm, drawing him back the way they had come so he could see his grandson. 'So, teach him. Show him how to be better.'

They watched the woman twirl a small lock of hair in her fingers as she spoke to Liam. He was trying to indicate towards Jerry, but the woman was not listening.

'You make it sound easy.' Jerry stared at Liam, his stance wavering. 'He does seem worried.'

'If you're not here, how is he going to learn to be a better man?'

'I suppose you might be right.' Jerry scowled at Ernie.

With a quick shove, Ernie pushed Jerry's ghost self towards his body before the man could change his mind. The light flickered and Jerry jerked upright, startling Liam and the woman.

'THAT WAS A DIRTY trick,' Jerry said, rubbing his knee. 'I wasn't ready.'

'Don't whine,' Ernie said half-heartedly. He hadn't told them how much worse it could have been, hadn't really explained at all to be fair. Neither seemed to want to ask, and Ernie was happy to leave it at that.

'What now?' Jerry asked, watching Liam flirt with the woman. She'd pulled him aside after Jerry had interrupted her. She slipped him a piece of paper, then smiled widely as she moved away.

Liam pocketed her number as he joined them, not giving Ernie a chance to answer. 'Can I have a minute, granddad?' Liam asked, glancing at Ernie nervously. 'In private?'

Ernie smiled, leaving them alone to talk, heading outside. He could already feel the summer's breeze that preceded Leigh's arrival. She was leaning against the wall.

'You're not going to make them forget?' she said, glancing at him with a raised eyebrow.

'There are enough things forgotten here already without removing any more memories,' Ernie said. He often thought being around so many old men must have stolen some of his sense. It was an excuse that Ernie would use frequently many years after he had moved on, as if 'old' and 'human' had been some kind of contagious disease. 'I doubt either will believe what happened after a good night's sleep. The human mind is strange.'

'Freyr. Are you sure you want to stay here?' Leigh asked, ducking her head. 'I think you might be getting sentimental?'

'Eir, I'm retired, see.' He pointed to the retirement home sign, Gard Village—Senior Living. Someone had added 'Mid' to the front of the sign in graffiti. It hadn't been him, of course. 'People who are retired get to be left alone.'

'You don't have to be alone,' she said, glancing at him when he said nothing. 'You can't hide here forever. What will happen will come regardless of what you want. You know this.'

He didn't look at her. She wasn't wrong, but he didn't want to argue with her about it. He had time yet. She shook her head.

'I'm here when you change your mind,' she said, pushing away from the wall, disappearing between one step and the next.

A few moments later, Jerry came out with his grandson, exchanging an awkward hug before he left to get in his car. Ernie had already handed over the keys.

'I will not miss that mop. The barber almost broke his scissors on it,' Jerry said as he patted his balding head.

There was a shout from the car, like a man being stabbed. The grandson sat in the front seat, the fedora in his hand. Ernie smiled as Jerry cackled.

Ernie knew he would have to leave one day. But it wasn't today.

Not My Problem

Author's Notes

I'm sure there are plenty of you out there who have heard these same words from your grandparents or parents... 'I was just resting my eyes.'

My granddad hated to admit he had fallen asleep in his chair. I remember once that he had been asleep long enough that the TV had turned off, and night had drawn in, but he'd always insist he had just shut his eyes for a moment.

Maybe it was because he was getting older, or maybe he just liked to argue—which he did. Regardless, it's a memory I hold close, and one that always brings him to mind.

Not My Problem

Magic pulsed through Ernie's skin with all the delicacy of a sledgehammer, slamming the doors of Gard Village—Senior Living opened with a loud crash. Ernie half expected lightning to flash in the doorway, but he was left disappointed.

If not for the ongoing poker game, the handful of residents that were in the communal living room might have glanced in the door's direction, but not much interrupted their game; especially not when Betty was playing. Any distraction would let her cheat.

The staff, however, were not quite so oblivious. 'Damn wind,' one of them muttered as the door slammed closed again. No one mentioned that the weather was mild for autumn, and there was not a breeze to be found outside.

Ernie sighed and set aside his book to wait.

The woman that finally entered was barely five feet tall. She had a stout frame and large, heavy-lidded eyes that found Ernie immediately. Her frizzy, shoulder length hair had mostly escaped the hairband she had tried to secure it with. He didn't recognise her form, but then that wasn't unusual. It was easy to change your appearance when you had magic. Ernie had chosen to look like he was an eighty-year-old man, right down to the hunched shoulders and white hair.

She slid into the chair beside him. The sofa should have sagged under the change in weight, but there was not enough life left in the cushion for it to make the effort. To say the place was run down was like saying the sun was hot. 'How's it going, Fr—'

'My name's Ernie here,' he said, cutting in, pitching his voice low. Just because no one had looked at them didn't mean there was any point in pushing his luck. 'Everyone here knows me by that name. What name are you using?'

'You're making this harder than it has to be.' She sighed, leaning back in the chair, glancing at the name tag she was wearing. 'Lottie will do, I suppose.'

'Lottie?' Ernie asked, giving her another once over, growing suspicious. She was wearing a retirement home uniform with a name tag that said Gard Village—Senior Living. There were no staff here with that name. 'Why are you here?'

'In a second. It's been a long journey; I just need a minute,' Lottie said, eyes closing as she crossed her arms.

He tried to suppress his irritation at her answer. 'Long' was relative, considering where she had come from. 'Why are you dressed like one of the staff?' he asked, glancing at the uniform again.

'Don't get your panties in a twist. I'm only visiting.' She didn't open her eyes as she spoke. 'I've got a message for you.'

Before she could say anything else, Sophie, one of the senior staff, stalked over, trying to loom over them. She failed. Even though she had tied her hair back in a severe bun, her heart-shaped face, upturned nose, and permanent dimples made it impossible for her to look anything other than an overgrown child. She compensated by being a distinctly unpleasant woman who lived and breathed the small measure of power her position gave her. 'Lottie, you're late.'

'I'm sorry?' Lottie asked, opening one eye.

'You're supposed to report to me on your arrival,' Sophie said, pulling back so she could cross her arms. 'An hour ago.'

'Report to you?' Lottie asked, her eyes narrowed, magic stirring.

Ernie kicked her. 'Sorry, Lottie, leg twitched.' He kept his eyes on Lottie as the magic dispersed. She gave him a sidelong glance, but stayed in the same slouch as before.

'I wasn't aware of the protocol,' Lottie said slowly, like she was testing the reaction to the words.

'Well, you are now. Get up, let's go. There is work to be done. I don't know what the previous homes have been like, but I will not have any of my staff slacking off.'

'Work?' Lottie muttered under her breath. Something passed over her face that Ernie didn't recognise, and he braced for Lottie to pull on the magic again. 'Of course, I am happy to help.'

Ernie stared at her in shock. Lottie doing work. Unheard of. She ignored him as she levered herself to her feet and followed Sophie's quick march. He really should have stopped her. But all he could do was stare after her until they disappeared out of sight.

LESS THAN AN HOUR later, Ernie watched Lottie following along behind another junior member of staff. Her eyes were half shut still, and she nodded more as if she was moving to the beat of her own music, rather than acknowledging the other woman's instructions. But Lottie was following. She hadn't just left.

He hadn't been able to catch Lottie alone long enough to find out why she was here.

'Did they come in?' Albert said in what he probably thought was a whisper. He was a bald man, with a skeletal thin build and a preference for shorts despite the weather.

'Yesterday,' Donald said, waving his arm dismissively. He was as bald as Albert, but that was where the similarities ended. Hawk nosed, and with enough weight to make two of Albert, he took up half the sofa on his own.

Ernie tried to lean around the pair to watch Lottie. She was being too meek and accepting. Something was wrong.

'Good, good.' Albert rubbed his hands together. 'Betty won't have any idea. She's going to love it.'

Lottie tried to take a seat as the woman she was with stopped to talk to a resident, but before she could park her butt, the nurse was moving again. Ernie felt the stir of frustration across the room, but not actual magic. She just followed behind.

'What about the music?' Donald asked. Ernie tried to tune them out.

He leaned the other way as the two women headed to the nurse's station. Were the two women moving slower than before?

'Ernie, does that sound good?' Albert said, giving him a nudge.

Ernie blinked at him. He had lost track of the conversation. 'Sure,' Ernie said, trying to sound like he had been paying attention.

'Great, she'll never suspect you.' Albert smiled as he stood, rubbing his hands together.

Ernie opened his mouth to ask, but Albert was walking away. Donald took longer to get out of the chair. 'What did I agree to?'

Donald's dentures almost escaped as he laughed. 'The music.'

'For what?'

'Betty's party,' Donald said, frowning as he straightened. 'The one Albert is throwing?'

Ernie rubbed his eyes. He did not need this right now. 'I thought that Jerry was playing his guitar?'

'He's not feeling well.' Donald shrugged. 'Don't forget about the song.'

Ernie waited, but Donald just stared at him. When the silence veered into awkwardness, Ernie finally asked. 'Which is?'

Donald smirked, lowering his voice into a poor imitation. 'Can't help falling in love.' He might have tried to twitch his hips in a dance, but either age or weight hid the movement.

Ernie scowled after Donald as he walked away. Ernie was not going to sing.

He glanced at Lottie, where she was just visible inside the nurse's station. The two women had settled into chairs and Sophie was nowhere in sight. It should be safe enough to leave her for a minute while Ernie found out what could have made Jerry miss the party. Then he could deal with Lottie.

THE COMMUNAL LIVING ROOM led out onto a corridor that ran around most of the building. Jerry's room was a short walk away. His door was open as Ernie approached it. Jerry was laid up on the bed facing a TV. It droned quietly, too quiet for Jerry to hear as colour flashed on the wall.

Ernie stopped in the doorway, but Jerry never glanced away from the TV. He was a squat, stocky man with a few wisps of hair left on an otherwise shiny bald head. His large, bushy eyebrows made up for the lack of hair where they were set in a permanent scowl that half buried his eyes.

'Jerry,' Ernie said, calmly. Jerry looked perfectly fine, but Ernie was not going to jump to any conclusions.

Jerry turned to him and raised a bushy eyebrow. 'What?'

'What are you doing?' Ernie crossed his arms, giving the TV a pointed look.

Jerry blinked at Ernie, then turned back to the TV. 'I'm having a nap. Can't you tell?'

'You need to set up the music stuff for tonight,' Ernie said, trying to keep his tone even. He was not asking. He was telling. 'You said you would play.'

'Not my problem,' Jerry said, yawning, giving him another brief look. 'Someone else can do it. I just need a rest.'

Ernie stared at him. Jerry was known to be grumpy, belligerent, and occasionally outright rude. He was never lazy. Never couldn't be bothered.

'Was that all?' Jerry asked, but he had already turned back to the TV that he couldn't hear.

'Did you meet the new nurse, Jerry?' Ernie asked. He absolutely did not growl.

'Lottie seemed nice,' Jerry said, yawning again.

Ernie said nothing, spinning on his heel as he stalked away. He had not felt any magic. Not even a hum. But he had no doubt that was what this was.

Lottie was alone in the nurse's station when Ernie got back to the communal living room. She held a cup of tea in her hands, delicately taking sips.

'What did you do, Lottie?' He kept his voice low. Though there were a handful of people about, they were all looking as sleepy as Jerry.

'It's far too much work with all these people, Ernie,' Lottie whined.

'You could have left. At any time,' Ernie said. Lottie just blinked at him slowly as she considered what he'd said.

'I thought it might be fun to try working here. I was wrong. I'm very tired, Ernie. This is actual work.'

'Then why are you still here?' Ernie asked, fighting the urge to raise his voice.

'There is no need to yell,' Lottie said as she put her cup down and folded her arms, chin down, and eyes averted. She looked annoyed, but there was still no sense of magic from her. 'I sent the other woman away; I have to stay until she comes back.'

'Sophie?' Ernie looked around, though he knew he hadn't seen her.

'No.' Lottie snorted, chuckling to herself. 'She's got the constitution of a train. She's rushing about somewhere like a good little worker bee. Far too much energy.'

'Lottie, who did you send away?' Ernie did another survey of the room, but the place was big enough that it would take time to do a count of all the staff.

'The nurse. I borrowed her uniform.'

Ernie stared at Lottie, mouth open. He had assumed she'd made the outfit and the form. But borrowing from someone else was a lot less work. If there was one thing Lottie was good at, it was avoiding work. 'Where is she?'

'Home. Probably.' Lottie waved a hand. 'She's probably sleeping. Lucky cow. I should be sleeping, you know. It's way past when I normally nap.'

'Ernie, thank God, I need a favour,' Archie said. Ernie could see him shuffling towards him from the corner of his eye.

He was about to tell Archie that whatever it was could wait, but Lottie had closed her eyes, her head tilted forward. Relaxed in sleep. He swallowed the curse that was on the tip of his tongue and turned to Archie.

'Can you cook?' Archie said, face straight, desperation oozing out of him.

'Why?' Ernie already suspected he knew the answer.

'Norris was supposed to pick up the cake, and he forgot.'

'Let me guess, he's not feeling up to it?' Ernie said, glaring towards Lottie. Magic or not, she was affecting the people here, and it was spreading.

'Please, can you get one?' Archie wrung his hands together. 'I can't bake.'

'I'll figure it out,' Ernie said, exhaling slowly. He did not add that he could also not bake, deciding it probably wasn't helpful.

'Thank you. I owe you for this. I need to go get the decorations,' Archie said, smiling widely, as he turned and shuffled away.

Ernie gave Lottie another glance. She was still sound asleep. There was even drool gathering at the corner of her mouth. It was impossible to wake the woman once she had fallen asleep. Standing here with her wasn't helping. Maybe if he found out why she had come, he could get rid of her, and the lethargy she was spreading.

He might not be able to get answers from her, but he knew where he could. Gritting his teeth, he left her where she was slummed and headed out. Maybe he could pick up a cake at Hel's house?

HEL'S DOMAIN HAD ALL the warmth of winter. Much of the same colours too. Blues and greens made the walls look like they were made from ice. The floor was a purple so deep that only the darkest night of winter would bring the colour forth. She had put small decorations about the place. Torches that burned with every colour other than yellow, and rugs made from thin spun glass. It cracked as he stalked over it.

Music pulsed around him, some upbeat pop song that the humans were into. Its pace was fast and energetic, with a deep base beat that he could feel through his feet. Everything about the place was beautiful, overdone, but beautiful. It looked entirely different since his last visit.

Ernie walked down the corridor with his senses open wide. He drew a few odd looks from the people who were scampering about. Mostly—and he only realised as he hit the ballroom—it was because he was the only person in the place who was not wearing formal wear. Several people in the room paused to stare at him.

Ernie took a moment to stand under their attention. His beige trousers and knitted cardigan did not have the same effect as the diamond dress, or the spider silk shirt. But it definitely made an impression.

Dozens of people danced around the room, moving with energy and grace. He ignored them and headed straight towards Hel. She was easily found in the centre of the room. Her dress was long and flowing, made of half of water and half of ice. Her skin was an inhumanly pale tone, her hair a purple so dark, it was black in most light. She was swaying to the beat of the music, people dancing around her. She opened her eyes slowly as he approached her.

'So good of you to visit.' Hel put emphasis on the word visit, her eyes changing to a different winter colour with every blink.

'I—'

'Without an invitation,' she continued, as if he hadn't spoken.

'Hel—'

'Or the proper attire.' Hel took a glass of what was probably wine. It glowed with a light of its own.

Ernie crossed his arms, waiting for her to get past the drama.

'Why are you here, cousin mine?' she said, sighing, waving her hands at the surrounding people. They moved a short distance away from her.

'Your handmaiden has got distracted; I want you to call her home.' He tried to sound at least a little respectful. It was not polite to insult the host, or the ruler of the land you were in. He was pretty sure he failed.

'My handmaiden?' Hel smiled slowly, taking a sip from her glass with feline grace. She looked over at the small crowd of women who were never far from her. 'Oh dear. It looks like you're right. One of them is not here.'

Ernie rolled his eyes at her. 'Call her home.'

'She's not needed tonight,' Hel said, voice sharp.

'Not needed? She's your handmaiden,' Ernie said, the words almost getting stuck as he spluttered. A couple danced past them, spinning with energy and passion. He watched them, realising for the first time how different this party was from the previous ones he had attended here. 'You sent her away?'

'She's so dreary. She drags everyone down. The parties are so much better when she is not here,' Hel said, moving her body in time to the beat. 'Can't you feel it?'

Ernie stared at her opened mouth. No wonder Lottie was avoiding returning, if this was how her own people were treating her. 'She isn't that bad.'

'She makes people sleepy, Ernie,' Hel said, rolling her eyes. 'Sleepy people can't party.'

Ernie scowled. 'So, you sent her into a retirement home with a bunch of old men and women who are already so sleepy that getting up is already a chore?'

Hel shrugged. 'They are at the end of their lives. Do you not think they deserve rest?'

Ernie exhaled slowly, then spun away from the woman without giving her an answer. Hel was wrong, and it was not up to her to make that choice.

With a boss like that, it was no wonder Lottie was not in any hurry to leave; she knew she wasn't welcome. Her attitude suddenly made a lot more sense.

As Ernie stalked back through the building, he had to reluctantly admit Hel wasn't exactly wrong on one point. Sleepy people did not make good parties. If he couldn't make Lottie leave, how was he going to make Betty's party a success?

One thing was for sure, it would not be by kicking her out. Not after this.

PEOPLE OFTEN SAY KNOWLEDGE is power. Sometimes that was true. Today, not so much. Knowing why Lottie was lingering didn't help get the residents of Gard Village moving.

He entered the building and had to fight through a wave of drowsy, no-hurry energy that hung over everything. It wasn't magic as such, he realised, it was just Lottie. Who and what she was affected everyone around her, including herself.

Lottie was awake again, slumped in her seat, listening to Sophie lecture about duty and work. Lottie took it placidly, not arguing. Ernie stopped at the door, watching them closely.

Sophie paused mid rant to almost, but not quite, glare at him. 'Ernie, dear, may I help you with something?' Sophie used the word dear like it was a warning, not an endearment.

Ernie smiled at her. 'Lottie offered to help with the surprise,' he said.

Sophie's eye twitched. 'Did she now?'

'Yes, she did. I really need her help now.' He stared at Sophie, unmoving.

'Very well, when you're done, report to me, Lottie,' Sophie said before she stalked away.

'You want my help?' Lottie seemed a little confused and lost by the idea. She shook her head. 'No one wants my help.'

'There is a surprise party,' Ernie said, wincing inside at the way her eyes widened. 'I need a hand with the prep.'

'I'm not very good at parties.' Lottie looked down as she said it, her voice small.

'That makes both of us.' Ernie nodded towards Donald, who was sitting in a chair at the far side of the room. His double chins folded under him like an accordion. 'Let's start with the basics.'

Donald did not wake as they approached him. It took several nudges, and a few shouts before he opened his eyes. 'I wasn't asleep.'

Lottie blinked at him. 'Yes, you were.'

'No, I was just resting my eyes.' Donald yawned.

'Where are the decorations?' Ernie said, interrupting Lottie before she could argue with Donald. Ernie had seen Donald fall asleep mid conversation before and still deny it.

Donald blinked slowly in the way of people who are about to lie but don't yet have all the details. 'Decorations?'

'For Betty's party.'

'Are you sure we really need them?' Donald shuffled in his chair, getting more comfortable, eyes closing a little. 'I'm sure no one will notice.'

Lottie sighed. 'He's probably right.'

'No,' Ernie almost shouted. Then grit his teeth, lowering his voice. 'Get up, you have work to do, man.'

'But there is no cake, no music. Decorations are just going to go to waste.'

'There will be both,' Ernie said, standing a little straighter. Cake. He had to get a cake. He'd forgotten. He turned to Lottie. Her shoulders were sagging, and her arms were crossed over her stomach. 'I need you to organise the decorating, Lottie.'

'What?' Lottie squeaked; eyes wide.

'Yes, organise.'

'No one has trusted me to organise anything, Ernie,' Lottie said it the same way that other people said there was a shark in the water.

'Then prove them wrong,' Ernie said, watching Lottie's eyes brighten. Donald stretched in his chair, leaning forward. 'Let's throw a party.'

Lottie's eyes flickered between Ernie and Donald, debating. Slowly, she nodded. 'Yes, yes. I can do that.'

'Good.'

'Where are you going?' Lottie called after him as he spun and stalked away.

'To see about a cake.' Ernie didn't look back.

THERE WERE MOMENTS IN his life that Ernie was never quite sure were real. As he stood in the centre of the metal kitchen, this was one of them.

The cookbook was open on the counter, and he had skimmed the instructions. Scales, bowls, sieves, knives and spoons were all piled in front of him. He wasn't exactly sure what they were for yet, and the instructions had not listed the knives, so he had gathered a variety of sizes, just to be sure he had everything he needed.

Albert had helped locate the ingredients. The first box of eggs had been more fragile than expected, but someone would clean that up later.

He was ready. They could do this.

'I've never seen anyone use a carving knife to bake a cake before,' Albert said over his shoulder. 'Or a butcher's knife. Are you sure you read the instructions?'

Ernie turned to glare at the man.

'I'm sure they must be needed,' Albert said, holding up his hands as he backed away a step, but he looked at the book again and sighed. 'And you're sure we shouldn't ask one of the staff for help?'

'I can make a cake,' Ernie said with confidence. 'Hand me the flour.'

Albert passed him a box of white dust. Ernie shook it towards the bowl and handed it back, waiting for the next ingredients.

'Eggs,' Albert said, placing a couple of eggs in Ernie's hand.

Ernie placed the eggs in the bowl and waited.

'I think you're supposed to break them?' Albert said.

Ernie smiled, picking up the butcher's knife, giving the egg a sharp tap, then stirred it slowly. He gave Albert a look. 'I told you we needed the knife.'

Albert made a choking noise as he half turned away. He eventually said, 'I don't remember cakes being that kind of crunchy, Ernie.'

Ernie stared at Albert as he continued to stir. The crunchy sound was surprisingly soothing. It definitely felt like the right way to make a cake.

'It's probably the baking that fixes it,' Albert said after a moment.

They continued, adding the butter, milk, and sugar until the mixture was a gruel-like consistency.

'It says it needs twenty minutes in the oven,' Albert said, peering at the book, then the oven.

They placed the mixture in the oven, only slopping a small amount over the edge.

'I think that went well,' Ernie said, crossing his arms. The glass bowl had fit once they had taken the rest of the rails out.

'I am not sure the staff will agree,' Albert said, looking behind them at the worktop. 'That seems like a lot more mess than I remember when my wife used to bake.'

Ernie ignored him. They had more or less followed the instructions. Nothing had mentioned cleaning.

'Next. Music,' Ernie said, spinning towards the door, inordinately proud of himself.

'Should we leave the cake alone?' Albert glanced at the book again.

'Does it need company?' Ernie asked. 'I'm sure it would prefer privacy to become its true self.'

Albert blinked at Ernie. Opened his mouth, then closed it. 'I never thought of that. That will be why the wife always shooed me away when she cooked.'

'Good. Let's get Jerry,' Ernie said. He wasn't taking no for an answer this time.

JERRY WAS STILL PRETENDING to watch TV, lying in bed.

'Time to get up,' Ernie said from the doorway.

'I told you—' Jerry broke off mid-sentence as he turned to Ernie and Albert. His eyes moved from their feet upwards in a slow suspicious look that old men somehow have perfected, usually towards the young. 'What happened to you?'

Ernie looked down at himself. Some white powder had stuck to his cardigan, and a layer of creamy gunk had coated half an elbow.

'Ernie baked Betty's cake,' Albert said, smiling widely.

Jerry pushed himself up and swung his legs over the edge. 'Ernie can bake?'

'It's unique.'

'Do I have to eat it?'

'I wouldn't risk it,' Albert said, voice solum.

Ernie scowled at them. 'Enough. Let's get this party ready.' He turned and stalked away before either could answer. 'My cake will be fine,' Ernie grumbled under his breath.

There was a part of Ernie who had been sure that Lottie would be asleep in the corner when he returned. But he was wrong. The decorations were up in a dizzying array of colour and paper in golds and reds. All the shades of warmth and a cosy fire. Somehow Ernie doubted that it was an accident that the colours were the opposite of Hel's.

Lottie was standing in the middle of the room, arms spread wide. Donald snored in the corner; a few decorations covered his stomach where he had been in the process of sorting them.

'These are even better than mine,' Albert said, grinning, patting Jerry on the back.

'You like?' Lottie asked, voice quiet, some of her pleasure dissipating as if she was expecting to be scolded.

'It's perfect, Lottie,' Ernie said, offering her a genuine smile. She beamed at him.

'Everything is ready,' Albert said, eyes going to the door like he expected Betty to walk in any second. 'Now we just need the guest of honour.'

'I DON'T KNOW HOW they do it,' Lottie said, moving to lean on the wall next to Ernie with a sigh. The party was a success. Betty was swaying to the music while Jerry plucked away on his guitar. Age had slowed his fingers, and made it hard to play, but he was in good form tonight. 'I can feel their tiredness. The weight of it. Even with me here, they still move, still dance. Still want to take part.'

'Age changes the body, not the mind,' Ernie said. Smiling as Albert invited Betty for a dance.

'I want this,' she said, voice quiet, smile slipping. 'This sense of belonging. It feels like family.'

'Who says you can't, Lottie?'

'I'm Sloth, the lazy slumber after a good meal. It's who I was made to be,' Lottie said, eyes down. 'Hel's handmaiden. The unwanted extra wheel.'

'You're not unwanted,' Ernie said, making sure she was looking at him as he said it. 'Hel is one person.'

'I'm tired, Ernie,' Lottie said, but there was a fire in her eyes that had been missing when he had first seen her. 'I don't know if I am ready to do something new. To leave?'

'Every single person here is tired, Lottie. Every day it's a chore to get up, get moving. But they do it anyway.' Ernie watched Donald get up and offer his hand for a dance to one of the women. 'Change can be good.'

'They're human, Freyr,' Lottie said, using his true name. 'We don't have the same adaptability of change and you know it.'

'Once, maybe,' Ernie said. Eyes drifting over the crowd. 'I baked a cake today.'

Lottie's eyes darted to the two-tiered cake, strawberries and cream decorated it. 'Where is it?'

'Oven ate it.'

Lottie frowned at him, half smiling. 'I was not aware that humans had made ovens that did that?'

'Stranger things have happened.'

Lottie laughed; it was a sound he had rarely heard from her. 'Maybe.'

They were silent for a minute, enjoying the feel of life the room gave off.

'Did Hel give you her message?' Lottie asked.

Ernie blinked at her in surprise. He'd forgotten that she had been sent here for a reason.

'She wanted to remind you it's almost time,' Lottie said. Ernie scowled at her. She raised her hands in mock defeat. 'I know, I know. I'm just passing the message on.'

'You and everyone else,' Ernie said. 'I have plenty of time left.'

Time For Change

Author's Notes

THIS IS THE LAST Ernie Smith and the Seven Deadly Sins story. That isn't to say that there won't be more Ernie stories in the future—there likely will be—but this closes off this series and characters. It's been a blast writing them and making this tribute to my grandad's quirks.

Thank you for buying and reading these stories, and I hope you enjoyed the journey as much as I did.

A huge shout out to my writers' group: Sabrina, Sarah, and Grace, who have helped me edit, and knock this entire series into shape.

TIME FOR CHANGE

A horn blasted through the communal living room of Gard Village—Senior Living. It held an unnatural weight and depth, as if it was everywhere at once.

If Ernie had been human, his heart might have skipped a beat at the overly dramatic sound.

'What the hell was that?' Abraham asked, shouting. When Abraham, who had long since decided he didn't really need his hearing aids—even though he clearly did—could hear it, you knew it had to be loud.

He wasn't alone in asking the question. More of the residents gathered, looking at each other over the threadbare seats and peeling tables, voices raised.

None of them had an answer, but it wasn't likely any of them were going to recognise Heimdall's horn. Ernie, however, knew exactly what it was, and it wasn't welcome. He stood, slipping through the growing crowd of residents.

'It's a horn,' Jerry said. The bald, squat man raised his heavy eyebrow at the room and the series of eye rolls. A small grin curled his lips, clearly showing he was enjoying winding the room up. 'What? He asked what it was?'

Ernie slipped out the door and headed towards his room without a word as the predictable argument started. It was safer this way. There was too much temptation to tell his friends the truth. But that wasn't fair to them. Knowing Ragnarök was coming wouldn't help them.

Hell, it wouldn't help him.

The sound came again, sending the hairs on Ernie's arm to attention like they wanted to march off. He rubbed at them, annoyed. One blast would have been enough. The last thing this world needed before Ragnarök was more magic floating around.

Because who didn't love a warning to the end of days?

Ernie paused as he entered his room. All the books from his bookcase had fallen to the floor. The hourglass that he had been so careful to take from Death stood upright on a shelf alone. The sand was now almost gone, with just a few little grains remaining. His time was up.

The horn sounded again.

'Yes, yes. I heard you the first time. No need to keep blasting the bloody thing,' Ernie shouted, though Heimdall was probably enjoying himself far too much to be listening. Like a child with a new toy, tooting away.

Ernie shook his head and picked up the hourglass. None of the sand moved as he turned it the other way up.

Wishful thinking, he thought.

'What's that?' Jerry asked from behind.

Ernie didn't jump. He was a God, and Gods did not jump when a human snuck up behind them. Not even on the eve of Ragnarök.

'Nothing,' Ernie said, turning to give the balding man a short glare, but it was hard to muster the spirit behind it. This would be the last time he got to glare at the man.

'Are you okay?' Jerry asked. He had one of his bushy brows raised now, like a caterpillar having a stroke.

The question was unexpected and sincere. He wanted to tell Jerry that it was far from okay. But it wasn't like Jerry knew what Ernie was or what the sound of the horn meant. Jerry was just asking a normal, human question.

'I'm fine,' Ernie said, realising he had been quiet too long. The horn sounded again, coming from everywhere and nowhere. The hourglass in his hand vibrated, so maybe nowhere wasn't exactly true. Ernie wondered if he threw the glass into a deep hole whether the sound would follow it? It was tempting just to see Heimdall's reaction.

Jerry frowned and looked over his shoulder. 'Where the hell is that noise coming from?'

Ernie was going to miss Jerry.

Or maybe not. After all, Ernie had read the prophecy just like everyone else. He might even have helped write it. Who remembered those details anymore?

Ernie was going to die during Ragnarök.

Stupid to have given away the sword that could have saved him, and in hindsight, not worth it. Especially not when marriage had turned out to be nothing like he'd expected.

'Abraham thought he might know,' Ernie said, the lie weighing heavily on his tongue. But it was that or say goodbye. And that was something he couldn't bear to do.

Jerry turned back, raised his eyebrow again, letting Ernie know that the lie hadn't been successful, but he nodded slowly, and left, giving Ernie space.

Even knowing he wouldn't make it, he was going to miss Jerry, miss all of them.

With a sigh, Ernie put the hourglass in his pocket and gave his room one last look. It held old worn furniture, with various random pieces of his life strewn about. If this part of Earth survived what came next, would someone here wonder where he had gone?

Ernie shuddered and turned away. He couldn't be here now. He didn't like the way it made his chest feel like he was being crushed.

But he also wasn't ready to answer the call.

Fortunately, there was another place he could go, even if just for a little bit.

THE RABID RABBIT WAS not a large pub, but it was exclusive. Well, it excluded anything that was human, at least.

It was in an out of the way section of town, done up nice'ish with new tables, chairs, and a rather sturdy looking wooden bar. The walls and floors were an old stone that hummed with the magic that had built up over time.

Ernie picked up the new glass of luminous yellow liquid that had been put in front of him and downed it, then stacked it to join the other four glasses. Not those piddly little glasses the humans used for shots. But the real size, whisky glasses. Even if the bartender wasn't filling them to the top, it made Ernie feel better.

'Another round?' the bartender asked, holding up the bottle of yellow liquid. It wasn't alcohol, but it would give him a kind of equivalent buzz.

Ernie squinted at the bottle, trying to remember how many he'd said he was going to have before he left. Another one wouldn't hurt, he decided as the horn pierced his ears. He nodded at the bartender, and the man poured the liquid into all five glasses for him.

Someone at the back of the bar stool, muttering under his breath, then stalked out. Ernie ignored him; the man wasn't the first to have left. Apparently, everyone found the sound annoying. He'd have to remember and tell Heimdall.

'Thanks,' Ernie said, smiling at the bartender. Ernie was pretty sure the words didn't come out right. But the bartender smiled as Ernie reached for the glass, so it must have been close enough.

A hand appeared on top of the glass, stopping Ernie from picking it up. Ernie struggled to follow it back to its source. Then regretted bothering as he recognised the man.

Pierce was wearing a scarlet silk shirt, puffy in the sleeves, and leather pants. The Draug was a tall, skinny man even in his human form. With the glow of the fake-alcohol in Ernie's system, he struggled not to see the overlay of the bones under the glamour.

'I think you've had enough?' Pierce said, giving the row of glasses a long look.

'Not 'nough,' Ernie said, forcing his tongue to pronounce the words. He tried to move Pierce's hand, but it was already gone. The glasses had just disappeared.

That was very rude of them, Ernie thought.

The horn sounded again.

'Tell me that isn't what I think it is?' Pierce said, after the horn had finished. Heimdall was getting bored, Ernie thought. The blasts were getting shorter. Maybe.

Ernie looked at Pierce again. He was sitting beside him. At a table.

That was probably a bad sign, Ernie decided, since he didn't remember moving. He took out the hourglass, tapping it. Maybe it was the reason he was losing time? Maybe that's why the horn sound was getting shorter? As long as it was shorter for him, he didn't care.

Pierce took the hourglass away from him, giving him a wide-eyed grin as he turned the thing over.

'You sneaky little bugger,' he said, sounding impressed. 'Death's having a fit looking for this.'

Ernie shrugged. It was too much work to get the hourglass back, especially now that there were two of them in Pierce's hands.

'Wasn't helpful,' Ernie muttered, pain forming in the centre of his forehead as the bartender's concoction began wearing off. It was days like today he wished he was human, and truly able to lose himself in drink and forget for more than a few moments.

'Not helpful? Are you crazy? We have the hourglass for Ragnarök. Can't we just, you know, put more sand in it?

Increase the time on it?' Pierce asked, spinning that thing around. Not a single grain moved.

The horn sounded again.

'Take that damned thing somewhere else!' a man at the back of the bar yelled.

Ernie and Pierce both ignored the annoyed voice.

'It's an hourglass made with the sands of time,' Ernie said, the headache pounding harder. 'How do you propose we get more of that? It isn't like the stuff is lying around.'

'Oh,' Pierce said, deflating. He sat quietly in the chair, staring at the hourglass like it had the answers. Ernie already knew it didn't. Stealing the thing had done nothing. Ragnarök was here. Pierce tapped the glass, then looked up and added, 'What happens if you just ignore it?'

Ernie laughed, the sound lost as the horn blared again. Pierce winced, rubbing his ear.

The man who had yelled earlier got up. At first, Ernie thought he was going to stalk out like the others. Seven feet tall, and with more hair than skin, it was hard to tell what he was exactly. Maybe if Ernie hadn't drunk so much, he would have paid more attention.

The man slammed his hands down on the table, making Pierce jump. The hourglass flew into the air. Pierce tried to grab it. He almost got it, fingers brushing the glass, but the hairy man got there first, catching it, and throwing it away from them.

Pierce squeaked as the hourglass spun through the air, hitting the stone floor, and shattered.

Time stopped.

Rippled.

Then magic ripped through the room, bringing a wave of heat as it cut off the horn.

ERNIE SPAT OUT A mouth full of sand as he tried to sit up. The fine white grains weren't making it easy. It was waist height in places, looking more like sand dunes than a bar.

'I think the hourglass heard you,' Pierce said, also spitting out sand. 'You think you have enough sand now?'

Ernie just stared at Pierce, not dignifying his words with an answer.

'No!' the bartender shouted, staring at rows of bottles of whisky that had turned clear. 'Not the Balvenie!'

Ernie winced; the whisky wasn't the only thing that had changed.

The man who had thrown the hourglass now lay on top of the sand. Or at least Ernie assumed it was him. A baby of less than a year old, with tiny hands and feet, reached into the air as he struggled inside the man's too large clothes. After a moment, the baby shimmered, turned into a bear cub, and started playing in the sand. Well, at least that answered the question of what the man had been.

Ernie forced himself to his feet, trying to grapple for balance on one of the bar's chairs that had turned into a tree.

Pierce looked down at himself, frowning. He'd not changed at all with the magic. 'That is not fair. I always wanted to look younger.'

Ernie snorted. Somehow, he doubted the man would have appreciated becoming a baby. At least Ernie was equally unaffected—they were both too old for the Sands of Time to affect them that way—except his hangover was now gone. Whether it would come back some day in the future, who knew?

Magic hummed through the room, and the bell at the top of the bar chimed with the arrival of a new guest.

'What the hell happened?' Vera asked from the entrance, mouth hanging open. Some of the sand poured out around her feet as it escaped the room. She was wearing the form of a young woman today, no longer the old hag he had seen her in recently. Verthandi suited the younger form better.

'It was him,' Pierce said at the same time as Ernie, both pointing at the bear cub digging in the sand. The cub paused to stare at them, then went back to playing.

'It's a pleasure to meet you,' Pierce said, trying to wade through the sand, but mostly just flopped forward.

Vera smiled, and closed the distance, moving gracefully over the sand like it wasn't there, so she could help him up. But since her power was over Time, specifically the present, she had an unfair advantage.

Pierce took her hand in his and dropped a kiss on the back of it. 'If I'd known Ernie's family was so beautiful, I would have had him introduce me sooner.'

'I'm Vera to my friends,' Vera said, giving a startled laugh, blushing. 'It's nice to meet you too.'

Ernie watched them continue to be awkward and strange as they made small talk. Neither noticed when the bear cub turned into a seven-foot-long adult bear, then into a naked, hairy old man. Ernie wished he could be as ignorant.

'Urth and Skuld are both freaking out,' Vera said, finally focusing on Ernie again. 'Though it explains why they were at each other's throats. You literally set past and future at war with each other.'

Ernie sighed. They wouldn't be the only ones affected. Great, something else they could blame him for.

'Are you okay?' Ernie asked. Vera was the embodiment of the present, there and then forgotten. Though Pierce seemed to be seeing her well enough just now.

She shrugged, giving him a quick smile. 'I'm fine. I actually feel great.'

'You better be planning on fixing this, Ernie,' the bartender said. He still looked the same, average, middle-aged man. He was clutching bottles that had now turned from clear to a much darker colour. Some smelled rancid. Tears filled his eyes as he clutched them.

'I didn't break it,' Ernie said, wishing for that fake-alcohol drink back. Was Ragnarök not enough of a problem for one day?

'If you hadn't been here, it wouldn't have happened,' the bartender said, putting the bottle down. 'I don't care how you do it, but fix it!'

CLEANING THE BAR TOOK magic. Mostly Verthandi's in the end as she sweet-talked Time into a bottle provided by the bartender. It compressed down almost as well as it had been in the hourglass. The biggest problem was that sand, even the Sands of Time, was still just sand, and it really did get everywhere.

It might have gone quicker if she and Pierce had not spent at least half of it staring at each other and blushing like teenagers.

By the end of the clean-up, Ernie was sweaty and itchy. He was not fighting Ragnarök with sand in his pants. Which meant he needed a shower and a change of clothes before he did anything else. Leaving Verthandi and Pierce to their flirting, he headed home.

He paused outside Gard Village and scratched his scalp. More sand trickled to the floor. He stared at it, sighing. Dragging a trail of sand behind him was going to bring unwanted questions. But no matter how much he tried to shake it loose, there always seemed to be more. The thought of going inside, even to shower, felt like so much effort all of a sudden.

'Ernie!' a familiar woman's voice broke him loose from his thoughts. He turned to stare at Lottie, squinting in the bright sunlight as she shuffled closer.

Lottie was wearing the same familiar form she'd been using recently. A frumpy, middle-aged, human woman whose hair looked like she had stuck her finger in an electric socket. Hel's handmaiden of sloth gave him a sleepy smile, either not noticing the sand, or not caring as she pulled him into a hug.

'How have you been, Lottie?' Ernie said, returning the gesture even though weariness weighed him down at the contact.

He'd become well practised at mitigating it after Lottie started visiting more regularly, but after everything so far today, it was an effort to shake off the effects.

'I've been great,' Lottie said as she pulled back, biting her lip. She might look sleepy, but it wasn't hard to see the worry under her heavy-lidded eyes and know what was coming next. 'I wanted to ask you something. About the horn.'

'Heimdall is probably still tooting it,' Ernie said, hoping the man took a long time to find out no one could hear him anymore. He would probably find another way for Ernie to hear the sound after that. 'The hourglass is broken.'

'It's stopped?' Lottie said, looking about as if she expected to find him with the horn, then she shook her head. 'But no, that's not what I wanted to ask. What if the rest of the signs just didn't happen? I mean Fenrir might not break free?'

'Ragnarök is here, Lottie. There is no stopping it. The wolf will break free, and the serpent will burn the world,' Ernie said, though the latter was more likely a metaphor. The Dragons didn't go around burning things anymore.

Lottie was silent as the wind picked up, tugging at the sand in his hair, making his scalp itch even harder. He wondered if he should have made his form bald. Then it wouldn't have had anywhere to bury itself.

'I've only just started finding my place,' Lottie said quietly.

'I'm sorry,' Ernie said. And he was. More than she would ever know. Hel had treated her poorly; he'd enjoyed watching her come out of herself and start to live.

'I should go,' Lotty said, looking away, then back at him. 'You will fight it, won't you? Prophecies aren't always right?'

Ernie could tell the last part had meant to be a statement, not a question. He nodded at her. 'Of course I will.'

It likely wouldn't matter. But he was going to fight.

'I'll see you later?' Lottie said, straightening. It was the most awake he'd seen her since he'd first met her.

Ernie nodded, unable to form an answer as Lottie spun away from him. Magic prickled his skin as she disappeared mid step. Something else she was getting better at.

Throat tight, Ernie turned back to the front door. He needed to be clean before he could fight. Then he could keep his promise to Lottie. Even if it was a fight he knew he would lose.

ERNIE HADN'T TAKEN MORE than a few steps inside before he heard a familiar voice.

'This is the best cake I have tasted in years. I should have visited Ernie sooner.' John's voice drifted to Ernie from the communal living room, holding the edge of panic that often happened when someone had been cornered by Betty.

'That's so sweet, my dear. You're welcome anytime,' Betty said, voice low and husky. 'Here, have some lemonade.'

Ernie almost kept walking. It was tempting. But the last time John had visited, things had not gone so well. Who knew being a Genie would be that hard?

With a sigh, Ernie turned towards the communal living room.

Betty had indeed cornered John. She was a slim woman whose age never seemed to wear her down. Silver hair flowed around her shoulders in a silky wave, and deep laugh lines curled around her eyes, marking a life of joy.

The other retirement home ladies stood between John and the exit, plates with chocolate cake and a pitcher of lemonade held out like spears to stop him from leaving. Somehow, they always seemed to arrive just as a young, attractive man appeared. And John was exactly that, or at least he looked it. Young, muscular, with a square jaw, and quick smile. Unlike Pierce, he knew exactly how to flirt.

John saw Ernie immediately, eyes pleading for rescue. 'Ahh, and here is the man now.'

Betty turned to Ernie. She opened her mouth, then closed it as she slowly looked him up and down. 'Have you been to the beach?' she asked.

Ernie scowled, taking another step into the room, then regretted it. There was sand in his shoes. 'No.'

'Thank you so much, ladies,' John said, taking the momentary distraction to manoeuvre his way out of the little semicircle. 'But I really must have a word with Ernie.'

The women followed for a few steps, but being seventy years and upwards, they couldn't keep up. Betty gave Ernie a disapproving look that he ignored. She always disapproved of young men escaping.

'We are starting a poker game soon if you want to join?' she shouted after them as John grabbed Ernie's arm and dragged him away.

Ernie let himself be pulled down the corridor towards his room, trying to shake off the disappointment that he might not get another chance to lose a game of poker with Betty.

'I'm not covering for you so you can take a holiday again, John,' Ernie said, tugging his arm out of John's grip, and setting a more sedate pace through the old off-white hallway; age had not been kind to the paint. Though the idea of being a Genie while someone else dealt with Ragnarök had an appeal.

'Hell no,' John said, looking over his shoulder. Only when it was clear the woman wasn't going to catch them up did John relax. 'I only just finished re-organising the mess you made.'

Ernie smiled, remembering his search for the tape to fix John's rule book. That book had never looked better. John's place, on the other hand? Well, that had seen better days.

'Then what do you want?' Ernie said, crossing his arms as he stopped to watch John. Clearly, he wanted something, or he wouldn't be here.

More sand trickled onto the floor at Ernie's feet. John's eyes followed it, mouth opening.

'Don't ask,' Ernie said through gritted teeth. He really needed a shower.

'I wasn't going to. I don't want to know,' John said slowly, but he stared at the sand.

'What do you want?' Ernie said again.

John blinked, looking back at him, giving him a too wide smile. 'I just wanted to catch up, have a chat, have a siesta.'

'A "siesta" is a break from the midday sun. Usually resulting in sleep, not talking,' Ernie said, crossing his arms, growing suspicious as John danced from foot to foot like a child on a sugar rush. John wasn't one to just stop by for a visit. He was here for a reason. Right now, there really was only one option. Ragnarök. 'Who told you?'

'I don't know what you're talking about,' John said, glancing around at the doors that lined the hallway. Rooms that belonged to the other residents. Simple people, living simple lives. That was all Ernie had wanted. Now it was over.

'I got it!' A woman's voice cried out, magic hitting him with all the grace of a bulldozer as she portaled herself into the corridor, almost taking out the wall. 'I told you it would be easy.'

'We got it, you mean?' another woman said, snorting. 'Don't you dare try to take all the credit?'

Ernie groaned as the magic dissipated, revealing two familiar young women. The first a young blond, and the second a brunette. Fin and Cara froze when they saw Ernie.

They shoved the sword that had been held out in front of them like a prize behind Fin's back, almost slicing Cara in the process. Neither of them was big enough to fully hide the blade. It glowed as if the sunrise was being reflected off the metal.

'Surprise!' John said, beaming as he waved his hand at the women and the sword. 'We got your sword. We got Sumarbrander.'

ERNIE SIGHED, RUBBING HIS face. All he succeeded in doing was scratching his skin with sand that still trickled from his hair.

'That's not Sumarbrander.' Even if it was, that sword wasn't his any longer, and while the trade had never turned out to be worth it, it had been made in good faith.

No one spoke, exchanging a series of glances.

'Yes, it is. We thought you would be happy to have it back, considering the prophecy,' Fin said, bringing the sword back around, no longer trying to hide it.

The blade was identical to Sumarbrander, beautiful, like Ernie remembered. But it had none of the energy or power of the true weapon. This sword wouldn't save him at Ragnarök.

Then it registered what the sword meant.

'Tell me you didn't steal this from Skírnirt?' Ernie said slowly, looking at all three in turn. It wasn't hard to imagine them stealing from anyone, even if it was the wrong sword. 'How exactly do you expect that will go down when he realises the sword is gone?'

'And on that note...' John said, taking a step backwards, clasping his hands together, '...I told them it was a terrible idea.'

'Hey, this was your idea,' Fin said, narrowing her eyes, taking a step forward.

John just continued to smile as he tipped an imaginary hat towards the women. 'Ladies.'

'Don't you dare—' Cara broke off as John disappeared.

The smell of chocolate cake filled Ernie's nose.

Fin spat. 'Arg. That's disgusting. Teleporting shouldn't have that kind of side effect.'

Ernie fought to keep his anger in check, failed, then turned and walked away. Being angry was better than the other emotion. His chest felt tight as he kept moving.

'Ernie, come on,' Fin shouted after him. 'Now you can fight at Ragnarök, and everything will be fine. You'll be fine.'

'I can't fight with that sword. Even if it was the real one, you stole it,' Ernie said, keeping his voice level. The hallway might have been empty now, but there was no telling when one of the other residents would decide to come out of their rooms.

'But John said—'

'John is a Genie. It's his job to skirt the line. Both of you should know better,' Ernie said, stopping outside his door. The pull of the shower called to him. 'Why are you taking his advice about Ragnarök?'

'Well, after Freya moved his bottle without his permission, he was trying to get back to her. We got to talking.' Fin shared a smile with Cara, which told Ernie that talking might have been stretching the truth just a little. She turned back to Ernie, letting the smile drop away. 'It was a good idea.'

Ernie rolled his eyes. Well, that explained why Ernie had ended up playing Genie. His sister really should find a hobby. 'It wasn't a good idea. I can't fight with a stolen sword. Go put it back.'

Without waiting for a reply, Ernie pushed open the door to his room, stepping inside with every intention of shutting the door in both the women's faces.

Pain lanced through Ernie's chest like lightning had been funnelled through him—heat and fire so bright he thought his body might burn up into ash. He stumbled back a step, grabbing the door frame, trying to find his balance.

'Did you think I would just let you steal one of my swords?' Skírnir said, pulling back, taking some of the fire with him. The magic was a familiar heat, something he hadn't felt in a very long time.

This was the real Sumarbrander. And Skírnir had just stabbed him with it.

The world tilted.

'What is wrong with you?' Fin said, voice distant. Someone caught him, the hands barely felt against the heat of his blade. 'You can't go around stabbing people.'

'I just did,' Skírnir said, voice holding a note of smug pride. 'Sumarbrander is mine. Fairly traded. Think yourself lucky. If I'd known it was you who had stolen it, Fin, I would have stabbed you instead.'

Ernie ignored them, focusing on the power that echoed out from the depths of the metal. The sword had fought for him in the past, with him like an extension of his arm. It hummed with displeasure now, unhappy with the way it had been used.

'Freyr is your friend.'

'And?' Skírnir said, snorting. 'It's not like he can die.'

'You stabbed him in the gut, with his own sword,' Fin said, voice close. The pain flared with movement. 'Shut the door before one of the humans notices.'

'Don't be ridiculous. Ragnarök is really specific about when he is going to die,' Skírnir said, but he no longer sounded sure.

Ernie tried to open his eyes, but it was as if someone had glued them shut. He didn't feel fear at the restriction, which was a surprise. Ernie tried to curse, but the words didn't quite make it out

Skírnir made a sound that might have been an insult.

'I'm calling Leigh,' Fin said, patting Ernie's hand, making the pain flair brightly. 'She's a healer. She'll know what to do.'

'You're not going to tell her I stabbed him? Are you?' Skírnir said, voice growing further away as if he had stepped back. When no one replied, he added. 'Ah, I just remembered I have to be somewhere.'

'No need to rush away, Skírnir,' Leigh said into the echo of a pulse of energy. The feel of the sword spiked at the new presence, as if checking for a threat. 'I can't wait to hear this explanation.'

LEIGH WASN'T IMPRESSED BY all the drama. Ernie could tell by the way she clicked her tongue, the sound sharp in his ear. That and the way she prodded her finger into the wound on his chest. It hurt distantly, like he was disconnected.

Ernie's vision was slowly coming back, and he was treated to a view of Skírnir standing near the wall like a sulky child. The man had taken the form of a man in his mid-thirties, with a weightlifter's build.

'It was a misunderstanding,' Skírnir said, eyes on the floor, sword now sheathed. Ernie could feel the power of it, like an itch in the back of his skull. He might have missed the sword, but not so much that he wanted it inside his chest. It hummed in agreement.

'I'm so very glad that after several thousand years of existence, stabbing people is still the result of a misunderstanding,' Leigh said, not looking away from Ernie as she adjusted a piece of cloth she had placed against his wound. The magic tingled like a thousand ants crawling around under his skin. She was in the same familiar form she often used—pretty, but not so much that people would stop in the street to stare. Against Fin, she looked downright plain.

Skírnir shuffled his feet. Ernie was quite enjoying watching the man squirm. He had to remember how Leigh was doing it so he could use it on Skírnir in the future. If there was time.

'He might be a God, but Ragnarök hovers on the horizon. What was immortal will die, and we all stand on the front line of change,' Leigh said, lifting the cloth to look at the wound on Ernie's chest. The pain was almost gone, along with the heat. 'It has been prophesied, so shall it be.'

'You say it like it's inevitable? We are Gods,' Fin said, holding Cara's hand tightly. 'You may be happy to walk into the hands of death, but I would rather fight it.'

'Everything has an end, even the world. Ragnarök is just an end to one cycle,' Leigh said, standing, wrapping the cloth up and tucking it into her belt. The blood faded from it like it had never existed. She turned to them, placing her hands on her hips. 'Now, I'm sure all of you have things to be doing with the final battle coming. So, off you go.'

All three tried to argue, but Leigh brushed away their complaints until they disappeared one by one. Ernie gave a sigh of relief, ignoring the sadness that always came when the sword's light disappeared from his presence. But it was good to have his space back. His room wasn't big enough for that many people.

'Thank you, Leigh,' Ernie said, scratching at the residual itchy sensation where the sword had struck him. It was no longer painful, but his skin crawled like it was still trying to fix itself. 'Was it necessary to let them think the wound was serious?'

'I enjoyed watching Skírnir squirm,' Leigh said, smiling widely. 'But you made it too easy by putting such a heavy glamour around yourself. The blood was a nice effect.

But you're damned lucky the sword didn't just shatter the glamour.'

'I don't think Sumarbrander knew what to do with it,' Ernie said, snorting. He had spent a long time building up that glamour, but it had never really been put to the test like that before. He would need to make some tweaks; the blindness and paralysis hadn't been part of the design.

If he had the chance to make changes.

The humour died almost as soon as it had come. He was out of time.

Leigh shook her head, giving Ernie a more serious look. 'Change isn't always bad.'

'Change maybe, but this isn't just change,' Ernie said, looking around the room at what he was going to lose. The battered furniture had become more of a home to him than any palace he had lived in. 'It's a reset.'

'Either way, it will come, and you must face it,' Leigh said, giving him a sad smile as she stood.

'I know. You sound like you've been speaking to my sister?' Ernie said, swinging his legs around to put them on the floor. He fingered the hole in his shirt and cardi. Between that and the blood, there was no saving it. Not that it mattered. He'd already intended on changing after his shower.

'I'll see you on the battlefield, Freyr,' Leigh said, using his true name. With so many Gods coming and going, the magic was as light as a feather as she disappeared.

'Soon,' Ernie said, standing. He looked down with a sigh. There was still sand in his damn shoes.

ERNIE CHECKED THE GLAMOUR of his old man's visage. It had become more familiar than many others he had worn over this lifetime. The human routine, shower and dress, the mundane actions that others had to follow. He'd hated it in the beginning, but now it was almost over. He regretted all the times he'd cheated.

With a sigh, he turned towards the bathroom.

'I didn't think you were the sort to give up this easily, Ernie.' Sky's voice was soft behind him.

He didn't jump. Though if he had, doing so because one of the best-known hunters had snuck up on him could have been considered a compliment. With the constant flow of magic from all the coming and goings, he hadn't felt her arrive.

'Don't you think the rest of them have made enough of a mess?' Ernie said, taking in the Amazonian blond. Sky made no effort to fit in, wearing aged animal skins, the fur belonging to creatures that have long since become extinct, and her head brushing the ceiling. The Giant rarely liked to stand to a human normal height.

Sky gave him a long look, lingering on the hole in his cardigan. She made him feel old for the first time in his life. Then she took in his bedroom. He could imagine what she was thinking. The same as everyone else who had come through here in the last few years. Why choose this place? Ernie didn't offer an answer. It didn't matter why it felt like home. Just that it did.

'That's because you're not the only one who is unhappy with the call to arms,' Sky said, crossing her arms. 'Did it ever occur to you to ask if others wanted to roll this dice? You might find they are equally not ready to begin Ragnarök.'

Ernie blinked at her slowly, considering her words. Was that even possible? Could they just say no? The others had all been trying to help, wanting things to remain the same. What if they weren't the only ones? Would it matter?

'It's not like I can just go talk to Hel. Somehow, I doubt she will want to talk to me while the horn sounds in the distance,' Ernie said, but the idea held. What if there was a way? Did Hel really want to fight?

Sky snorted, shaking her head. 'Honestly, Ernie, I sometimes wonder if you have become as senile as your form suggests. You do remember where I come from? It's not like Hel can invite all the other Giants and leave me behind.'

Sky's form shimmered like heat rising from the desert, a shadow of her true form filling the room. It didn't solidify, which was just as well. She would have taken out half the roof.

'You would talk to her?' Ernie asked as the magic settled back down, and Sky faded to her mostly human visage. Hel wasn't exactly known for her welcoming nature, and after everything with Lottie, he was not exactly in her good books.

'I can get you a meeting. The rest is up to you,' Sky said. Her clothes faded to a human style that would have fit in almost anywhere. A brown waist length leather jacket, and tight, pale jeans. 'I like my life here. I'm not ready to give it up either, Ernie, so you had better be convincing.'

Ernie grinned at her; the threat was unspoken, but no less present in her tone. He put his hand out to her, taking a step forward, the sand still rubbing his feet in his shoes. But a shower could wait.

Sky smiled and took his hand. Her magic was a feather light touch as she teleported between one blink and the next.

Rather than arriving at the entrance where he would normally end up, Sky had taken them into the centre of Hel's grand hall. And they weren't alone.

The room rippled with motion as Giants of various sizes and forms took notice of their arrival.

'Hel, I present Freyr, come to converse and cause no harm unto anyone present,' Sky said, her formal voice echoing through the room. The unnecessary introduction was more to pre-empt the overreaction that was already starting. 'I have assured him safe passage to complete this task.'

The half a dozen swords and axes slowly lowered as the crowd muttered, no one entirely sure what to do now. Ernie resisted saying anything. He was here to negotiate, after all. Being rude wouldn't help that.

Hel sat on a throne of ebony and ice, the arms curving in the shape of a warhorse, and the legs looking like the knees and arms of a human. Ernie didn't look too close to see if they were real.

'What right do you have to make that assurance?' Hel said to Sky, anger showing in the way the chair writhed, moving into a tortured position. 'Actually, never mind, I don't care.'

A Giant stepped forward, taking Sky's arm in a tight grip. She let him, though Ernie could tell it was an effort for her to stay still.

'I'm not ready to be done with this world,' Ernie said, addressing the Giants, ignoring Hel. 'How many of you can say the same? How many have made lives among the mortals?'

A mummer spread through the room, many whispering agreements.

'I have a wife,' a bald Giant said, stepping forward. He was in a human form, with heavy muscles. 'A life in the human world.'

'I just started a new job,' another woman said, her skin tinged blue. She looked out into the crowd. 'I worked hard to get it. I'm not ready to give it up.'

'Who will feed my goldfish?' a curly haired man said, voice breaking out from the others. Several people turned to him. Ernie could see them weighing the importance of goldfish vs the wife. Not everyone settled on the same side of that priority.

Other voices rose in the room, similar stories. Ernie was particularly fascinated by the one who was living as a pet cat in a mansion. Each to their own.

'Enough, this is not a debate. The horn has sounded,' Hel said. 'We are called to battle, and we will rise to the challenge.'

'Why?' Ernie pressed. 'Why is it the horn that decides when we fight? We are not bound by the threads of fate like humans, yet we rush to this one. Because of a horn? Because we were told that when it sounded, we would fight? What if the prophecy was wrong? What if the horn is sounding for another reason? *What if Heimdall is just bored?*'

Sky made a disapproving sound in her throat, but Ernie ignored her. She obviously hadn't spent enough time with Heimdall.

'It isn't just the horn, it is only the first of many events,' Hel said, then her smile grew in a slow curl of her lips like a lion before it pounced. 'Unless, of course, you can stop Fenrir from breaking free from his chains? Then I will not sail into battle with the Giants behind me.'

'Done,' Ernie said. That he had just told Lottie that such a thing wasn't possible only a short while ago made his stomach drop. He hadn't been wrong then.

Sky gave him a long look that told him she agreed with how stupid the agreement was. Fenrir was not like the reluctant Giants. He was chained, forever trapped, until

Ragnarök came. Only then was he fated to finally be free. There was no gain for the wolf to do nothing.

Ernie blamed too much time around humans for the hasty reply.

Hel raised a slim eyebrow, then nodded. That smile said she knew it was very unlikely Fenrir was going to stay chained.

Silence followed Ernie as he turned and walked out. The Giant didn't let go of Sky's arm, and while Ernie didn't doubt she could fight her way free, an army of Giants would be too much for even her. He was on his own for this one.

Maybe Fenrir was in a good mood. Stranger things had happened.

ERNIE HEADED TOWARDS FENRIR'S cave without any weapons. It wasn't because the prophecy of his death clearly did not involve Fenrir killing Ernie. It also wasn't because he was confident—he absolutely wasn't. No, it was mostly because Ernie's toe felt like the sand had rubbed it to the bone, and if he had to walk any more than the absolute minimum, he was going to lose his mind. Not that a weapon would help much against a wolf the size of a bus.

By the time Ernie finally made it to the cave, he was limping and debating if the old man's glamour was really worth it. A heavy weight of age settled against him, dragging him down. But Ernie had fought a great many enemies in the past and won. He was not about to be defeated by sand.

The cave itself was suitably atmospheric. Carved from onyx, the cave's walls and floors were a deep black with glowing algae spread like ivy over it, casting a greenish fluorescent glow over everything. It would've made a human stop and stare, but Ernie had seen more impressive structures.

'—you know what I mean?' The woman's voice was a surprise, and familiar. Ernie sighed, pausing to lean on the wall, his own sudden weariness making sense. But why was she here?

There was a long sigh of air, the strength of it becoming a gale that battered Ernie. 'I do, Handmaiden Lottie,' the wolf said, voice a whisper at the edge of a storm.

Ernie shook his head and continued further into the cave. Fenrir lay in the centre, easily the size of an elephant, his muzzle resting on his paws. With fur the colour of blood, and half-lidded eyes that shone with the same hue, he looked vicious. Hell, even if he had been normal sized, no one would have believed him a wolf. There was too much 'other' about him.

An onyx chain circled his neck, linking him to the walls. There was no visible join on the heavy links, like it had been carved, just like the rest of the cave. One day, Fenrir would break free from the chain. Soon. But right now, it looked perfectly fine, not a flaw in sight. It had lasted this long. Maybe it would last longer.

Lottie paced back and forth in front of Fenrir, steps quicker than Ernie ever remembered seeing before.

'No one ever understands—well, almost no one,' Lottie said, tucking a few strands of frazzled hair behind her ear. 'It's not my fault, really.'

Fenrir nodded his head a fraction, eyes closing almost entirely, then his nose twitched. The deep inhale pulled Ernie forward a step. He cleared his throat, making Lottie turn to him.

'Ernie,' Lottie said, giving him a wide, genuine smile. A yawn followed it, but that wasn't unusual for the hand-maiden of Sloth. 'It's so good to see you again.'

'Hel never mentioned you were down here, Lottie,' Ernie said, looking between Fenrir, who had lifted his head, and Lottie. Ernie wasn't sure who he should be more worried for.

'Oh, she doesn't know I'm here. She sent me away when the first batch of warriors arrived and they fell asleep,' Lottie said. 'I mean, it's not like it's really my fault.'

Her wide grin told him it was *definitely* her fault. Her control over her passive power was getting better now she was actively working with it. Being able to put people to sleep had its uses surprisingly.

Ernie looked at Fenrir, realising what Lotty had done as the wolf lowered his head back onto his paws. Never had Ernie seen Fenrir look so relaxed and calm.

This didn't look like a wolf about to break free and herald the end of days, but that wasn't to say it couldn't change, but hope rose. Maybe Ernie had a chance after all.

'Fenrir,' Ernie said, bowing his head to the wolf. 'You have heard the horn?'

'Who could miss it,' Fenrir said, another gale worthy sigh. 'Once would have been enough.'

'Heimdall really doesn't know when to stop,' Ernie said, forcing a smile. 'And do you intend to join in the hunt this day?'

'I'm tired, God of Summer. I do not wish to fight this day.' Fenrir's voice vibrated through the space, almost as if there was no source to the words. He turned to Lottie, giving her a wolf grin. 'I will converse with Lottie, if she would talk with me more.'

Lottie blushed, looking down at her feet as she wrung her hands together. 'I'd love to talk to you more.'

Ernie looked between the pair, Fenrir never looking away from Lottie while she kept sneaking glances at the wolf. Ernie wasn't going to pass judgement on what was clearly making them both happy.

'Shall I tell Hel that you are otherwise occupied?' Ernie said, focusing on Fenrir.

'Yes, yes, tell her this if you wish to,' Fenrir said, not looking at Ernie. 'Farewell, God of Summer.'

Ernie gave Lottie a smile as she glanced at him. She blushed again, but there was joy on her face that he had rarely seen. Ernie left them, walking back through the tunnel towards Hel's domain. He could barely believe what he had seen, what Lottie had done without any seeming effort.

Hel was going to have a fit.

ERNIE WAS ALMOST BACK at Hel's grand hall when he felt his sister fall into step beside him, appearing between one footfall and the next like she had been with him the whole time. The arrogance set his teeth on edge, but then, that's what twins were for.

Her long red hair was pulled back in an intricate plait, making her angular face look sharper. She wore armour, form fitting, emphasising the slim twenty-something body she'd appeared in. She carried no weapon, but they were in Hel's house and that would have been rude.

'I see you've finally come yourself,' Ernie said to her. 'You got bored with sending others to tell me time is running out?'

Freya smiled, giving him a sideways look. 'I never get bored.'

Ernie snorted. 'Why are you here?'

'You think I'll let my brother walk alone into Hel's hall alone after defeating the great Fenrir?' Freya said, almost managing to keep a straight face. Then her smile broke through and she laughed, nudging him with her shoulder. The armour rattled as it spread over Ernie, encasing him in a duplicate, and less flattering, version. 'I have to see her expression.'

Ernie shook his head, rolling his shoulders as the weight settled around him. In years gone past, he would have matched his sister in age and build. But not this time. He was here because he wanted to keep his life and home. This form was the one that would go into battle.

'Without Fenrir, there will be no Ragnarök,' Ernie said, wishing he sounded more confident. There were other factors, many of them. The wolf was only one sign.

'The serpent has not burned the world, and the sun rises as it should,' Freya said, shrugging. 'The hourglass was wrong.'

Ernie sighed. There was still sand in his shoes. Had breaking the hourglass before it had finished changed things? He didn't say it out loud as they entered Hel's grand hall.

There were no Giants in sight this time, and the room was almost empty, with Hel sitting on her throne in the centre of the hall, and Death standing to one side. He wasn't the only Death, but he was the one that covered Ernie's region, as well as the Death who used to hold the hourglass for Ragnarök.

Before Ernie had stolen it.

Death prided himself in being average in every way, height, build, hair, colour. But standing with his arms crossed, he looked plain, rather than average, against Hel's beauty. He knew it as well, going by the way he sent Hel an irritated glance.

'What is this?' Ernie asked, looking at the pair. The two working together gave him chills, especially since Ernie was the one in the wrong.

Death uncrossed his arms and pulled the familiar hourglass out of his pocket. It was in two pieces, and no longer held any sand. Ernie's head itched, like the sand there wanted to go back to its old vessel.

'I have been told that you know how the hourglass for Ragnarök has been broken?' Death said, eyes watching the few grains of sand fall to the ground from Ernie's head.

Rolling his eyes, Death tapped the hourglass. The sand tumbled forward towards him. It was only a few tiny fragments, but immediately the rubbing in his shoes eased off, then faded to nothing. Ernie scowled at them as they disappeared into the glass fragments. Bloody time magic.

Freya nudged him, raising her eyebrow. She looked impressed as she nodded at the shards. Death's stare grew colder. Ernie ignored her as he debated what he wanted to say. Lying, especially after that little display, wasn't exactly going to help him.

'Enough of this. Ernie is the one who stole the hourglass! Then he broke it to avoid his fate,' Hel said. Death turned that cold glare at her until she grew quiet.

'Yes. I'm aware he stole it. However, that is beside the point right now,' Death said, this time not looking at Ernie at all. Somehow, that felt worse. He was sure there would be another conversation coming in his very near future.

Death shook his head, and added, 'I want to know *how* it was destroyed?'

Ernie winced. He really didn't want to piss off Death any more than he had, but he doubted the truth was going to go down well. 'A mortal threw it onto the floor.'

Death's mouth thinned into a white line. 'A mortal shouldn't have been able to destroy a vessel of time.'

'Are you calling my brother a liar?' Freya said, voice dangerously low.

Ernie sighed, elbowing her in the ribs. The metal armour clunked. 'Not helpful.'

'You didn't break it!' Freya said, nodding at Death, glancing at the broken glass shards. 'What would you gain?'

Hel stiffened in her chair, mouth opening.

'One more word, and I will see to it that no one brings the dead to your domain for the next hundred years,' Death said, eyes never leaving Hel's. 'Freya is right. Ernie hasn't gained anything from today's events.'

Hel settled down; arms crossed like a sulking child. Ernie was impressed, and ever so slightly pleased, at the way Death dealt with her. Okay, he was very pleased.

But none of this was helping figure out what had caused the hourglass to break. Or why Death was so sure Ernie hadn't gained anything.

'We stopped Ragnarök?' Ernie said, unable to keep the question out of his voice.

Death laughed. The sound was surprisingly deep as it echoed through the room. 'You are amusing.'

Ernie narrowed his eyes at Death as he grabbed Freya's arm, stopping her from launching herself forward. She rattled to an abrupt halt, huffing an annoyed breath at him. Death didn't even acknowledge her.

'You didn't stop Ragnarök. Clearly, the countdown was wrong,' Death said, sobering up as he rolled the shards of glass in his hand, shaking his head. Death seemed neither pleased nor worried by the idea of the end coming. What would happen to the Deaths when there was no one left to take to the other side? Would they cease to exist? 'Ragnarök will still happen, but now only the Norns will see it coming.'

Whether Skuld would tell them was a whole other matter. Ernie hadn't seen her since he'd tried to convince her and her sister to take Vera back. It hadn't gone well.

Ernie exchanged a look with Freya. 'Skuld?'

'She wouldn't?' Freya said.

'If she was worried about becoming irrelevant?' Ernie said, thinking that sounded exactly like something the arrogant woman would do. 'She has the power to see the future, the only one who can see what's coming. Until they made the hourglass?'

Death's lips thinned, and the shards disappeared into his pocket. 'She hadn't been in favour of creating the hourglass.'

'It might not have taken much to change it, break it?' Ernie said, not that any of this helped them. Now the hourglass was broken. There was no way to be sure. It might also be another reason why Vera had said the sisters were at each other's throats.

'Well, I think it might be time to have a word with them,' Death said, giving Ernie one last stare. 'We can continue the other half of this discussion another time.'

Without waiting for an answer, Death disappeared.

Hel straightened in her chair, curling her lip. 'Don't think I will forget this.'

Freya smiled at the woman, taking a single step forward. 'Anytime you want to continue the discussion, I'm game.'

Ernie sighed and tugged on Freya's armour, turning back to the exit. She followed after a few heated glares at Hel. That was a fight Ernie didn't want to get in the middle of. Ragnarök would be the least of his worries.

Arriving at his room at the Gard Village—Senior Living, Ernie felt like he had come home. Freya had followed him. She stood, still in her armour, in the centre of his bedroom, looking around slowly.

'I'm not sure I get why you want to stay here,' she said. Shrugging her shoulders, making the armour disappear, replacing it with a green summer dress that echoed the colour of her eyes. Her hair fell out of its braid and hung in loose curls around her face. Ernie's armour dispersed as well.

'I like it,' Ernie said, kicking off his shoes. Though there was no sand now, they still ached from the constant rubbing. He sighed in relief, the pain easing already. 'It's normal.'

'There are a lot of types of normal, this is certainly an interesting choice,' Freya said, taking a seat at the end of his bed. 'Maybe I should visit you more and see if I like it.'

'You don't exactly fit in,' Ernie said, surprising himself at the spark of joy that his sister visiting gave him. He had been avoiding her for so long that he hadn't realised he'd missed her. 'But you are always welcome.'

Freya smiled. 'You have certainly collected an interesting bunch of friends.'

'You were the one who kept sending them my way,' Ernie said, joining her to sit on the bed. It was old, and uncomfortable, but it wasn't like he really slept, not like mortals anyway.

'Yes, well, they needed something to do. You have more patience with that than I do,' Freya said. 'Lottie and Fenrir, though, that was a surprise. Even to me.'

Ernie snorted. Trust his sister to take credit.

'What now?' Ernie asked her.

'Life goes back to normal.'

'Just like that?'

'Just like that,' Freya said, giving him a quick smile before she disappeared.

The silence was strangely comforting. Knowing Ragnarök wasn't still coming didn't worry him as much as he suspected it should. It was no longer imminent, and that was the main thing.

Ernie scratched his head as he stood. His normal was going to be getting a bloody shower to wash the itch the sand left behind before it drove him insane.

Then next, maybe Betty wanted to play poker.

There was a time for change, and today wasn't it.

A Long Dragon Day

Author's Notes

THIS STORY CAME FROM a submission request for a short story competition. I don't remember what the prompt was exactly, but I remember the idea it created. What would someone outside who's on the outside of a paranormal romance story think and do? Then, more specifically, how would Ernie deal with the romance drama and Alpha male arrogance often used in Shifter Paranormal Romance stories?

From that idea, this story was born.

A LONG DRAGON DAY

There was a Dragon on Ernie's doorstep.

'Please don't kill me,' the Dragon said in a rush. There was just time to read his name tag, 'Vinny', before it was hidden as he clutched his tool bag to his chest.

Ernie sighed, rubbing his forehead. All he'd done was say hello.

'I don't want to kill you, Vinny. I need you to fix the air conditioning,' Ernie said, managing a calm tone. Mostly.

Vinny kept his eyes down, refusing to meet Ernie's gaze. Considering that Vinny was a well-built man in his twenties that towered head and shoulders taller than Ernie, it might have been comical to watch. If it hadn't been the longest, hottest day of the year.

'I didn't mean to trespass,' Vinny said. His energy flickered against Ernie's skin like a candle flame, the heat barely registering.

'I'm not a Dragon.' Ernie gritted his teeth as Vinny flinched back a step. They were standing at the front entrance of Gard Village—Senior Living, and there was not a lot of space for him to retreat. If he went much further, he would be on the road. If that happened, Ernie might never get the air-con fixed. With a slow breath, Ernie tried to moderate his voice further. 'I'm not worried about who has what territory. I just need you to do your job.'

The staff hadn't noticed Vinny's arrival yet, but they would soon, and they were going to think it was odd that the young repairman was terrified of an eighty-year-old pensioner. Ernie's choice of body fit in well with the other retired people who lived here, but the masquerade came with its own restrictions.

'I didn't believe it was true,' Vinny said, shuddering. This time he managed to look up, pale eyes just short of meeting Ernie's before he looked away. Fresh sweat beaded on his forehead. Which, for a Dragon whose core was hot enough to belong in a volcano, was impressive. Of course, Vinny wasn't sweating because of the heat.

'Didn't believe what was true?' Ernie asked. He kept the spike of anger to himself. Frightened as Vinny was, he really might bolt.

New energy stirred, similar to Vinny's, but stronger, more confident. A bonfire on a still night. An Alpha Dragon. 'That there was a God living in a small-town retirement home.'

The speaker stood at the back of the repair van, where he had been waiting to see Vinny's reaction. Or Ernie's. Either way, the man was playing games. Well over six feet tall, with wide shoulders, and thick muscles that were on show like the cover of a romance novel—not that Ernie would read any such thing. There was no doubt this was where the power that Ernie had felt had come from.

Ernie suppressed the anger that the surprise brought, not just by the man's words, but that he had not sensed him sooner.

'You might still be wrong,' Ernie said. There was no way the Alpha could tell what Ernie was exactly; just that Ernie had power and was not a Shifter like them.

'And yet my senses tell me otherwise,' the man said. His eyes flared, colour turning gold. 'But you're right, of course. I could be wrong. It's not every day you meet a God.'

'I'm sorry, Tyler,' Vinny almost whispered the words, lowering his eyes.

Tyler moved forward to stand beside Vinny, putting a hand on his shoulder. 'It's okay, you didn't do anything wrong.' Tyler's voice was soft. It helped. Vinny no longer looked on the verge of bolting. 'I hadn't really believed the rumours.'

That anyone would have gone straight to God when describing Ernie was not ideal, but changing Tyler's mind did not seem likely right now. Besides, Ernie didn't like lying. So, he changed the subject instead. 'Why are you here? Somehow, I doubt you are the only repair company in town,' Ernie said.

Tyler smiled as he nodded his head. 'This retirement home skirts the edge of my territory.'

'That didn't exactly answer my question,' Ernie said. Tyler's smile dropped away, expression growing serious.

'Ernie, are these the repairmen?' a woman asked as she stepped outside to stand with him, sending him a disapproving look. The petite woman had not even hit her thirties yet, but she had already mastered that frown.

She turned to the Dragons and gave them a wide smile, showing off deep dimples. 'Hi, my name is Abigale. Please forgive Ernie. I'm glad you could come on such short notice. Let me show you where the unit is. It's been really flaky the past few weeks, but today it's just died. I really hope you can fix it. I can hardly believe the weather.' She spoke in a rush, barely pausing to breathe. She was the senior staff in charge of the retirement home today.

Vinny stared at Abigale as if he wasn't quite sure what to say to her. He glanced at his Alpha with a bemused look, his fear fading further as he was faced with her enthusiasm.

'I'll follow in a moment,' Tyler said, smiling at Abigale as he stepped closer to Ernie. 'Ernie and my father knew each other. If it's alright with you, I would like a moment to catch up?'

Ernie narrowed his eyes at Tyler's lie. Contradicting him was likely to cause more questions, so Ernie stayed silent. It didn't stop Abigale from sending a warning look in his direction, like it was him who had done something wrong.

'Sure, no problem,' she said, stepping onto the path that went around the building, squinting in the mid-morning sunlight. Indicating for Vinny to join her, she added, 'It's just this way. I'll show you.'

The two of them walked around the side of the building. Vinny managed to only look back once, but his nervous energy followed in his wake. Whatever Tyler wanted, Ernie wasn't going to like it.

'WHAT DO YOU WANT?' Ernie asked, tired of playing games.

Tyler's smile drop, as Vinny and Abigale moved out of range. This close, his energy sent tiny pinpricks across Ernie's skin. 'I would like your assistance for a negotiation. As a neutral party.'

'What part of me living in a retirement home did you not register? I don't do that stuff anymore,' Ernie said, then turned his back on the man and started to walk away.

There was nothing that would make him go back to those days. He was done.

'The part where I assume you would like your home to remain standing after the summer spins out on its longest day.' Tyler's voice didn't change in tone as he spoke.

Ernie spun back around, his own energy surging out in a wave that made Tyler take a step back, eyes widening even before Ernie spoke. 'Do not threaten me, boy.'

'Is it fixed yet?' a man shouted, forcing Ernie to reign in his temper before he did something Tyler would regret.

Taking a breath, Ernie turned to face the speaker. Jerry was a squat, almost bald man who was just on the other side of eighty. He stood in the doorway, arms crossed, and a scowl in full bloom.

'They're working on it!' Ernie shouted back at him.

'Well, make it snappy. Norris is threatening to take off more layers. He's already down to just his pants,' Jerry grunted as he turned to head back inside.

Ernie shuddered at the image as he turned back to the Alpha. It was hard to recapture his anger after that.

'I didn't mean it as a threat,' Tyler said, lowering his eyes, body stiff like the motion had caused him pain. 'But without your help, there will be a war when the sun sets tonight.'

Ernie shook his head in annoyance. 'I'm not part of your Dragon territorial games. Neither is this town.'

Tyler looked up, almost meeting Ernie's eyes. 'No, you're not. You are neutral, and you are powerful enough to ensure that both parties keep their bargains.'

Ernie rolled his eyes at the obvious attempt at flattery. 'Why will there be war?'

'The Blue Dragons took my mate from me.'

Ernie raised his eyebrow at the man. 'You do remember what century we are in, right?'

Tyler scowled at him. 'She chose me, and I chose her.'

'Except?'

'She is a Blue Dragon.' He looked away and when Ernie stayed silent, finally added. 'She is the daughter of their Alpha.'

'Who did not approve?'

'No. He claims I stole her and is refusing to let me speak to her,' Tyler said, barely containing a growl. 'Refusing to let her leave.'

Ernie scowled at Tyler. In this age, they really should have more sense than to pull this. Humans had come a long way in equality, and much to the Shifters' annoyance, it hadn't stopped there. But Tyler didn't seem afraid for her, just angry. Of course, that didn't make it right. 'The Blue Alpha has agreed to talk to you?'

'He has agreed to meet in a neutral location,' Tyler said, twisting his lips as he added. 'So he does not have to crush the Gold Dragon Flyte.'

Translation, this was their last chance before the war. If it came to that, the destruction would be extensive. While it was obvious Tyler didn't want to go to war, that didn't mean he wouldn't do it. He was gambling a lot on the idea that Ernie was powerful enough to keep the Blue Dragons in check. That implied a level of knowledge he shouldn't have, but that was a problem for another day.

'I will help you,' Ernie said, adding power to his voice so his next words held their own weight. 'But do not think that I am stupid, or blind, Tyler Windryder. You are playing a dangerous game, and there are ways other than negotiation to ensure that there is no war.'

Tyler nodded. Eyes were tight as he shuddered under the feel of the power and full name. 'I understand.'

ERNIE STALKED AROUND THE building, working to pull back his energy into something more human-sized. He should not have let out that much power. It was only going to draw more attention to him. Especially since there were already rumours about his presence. His retirement wasn't going to be quiet if every man and their dog knew where to find him.

Tyler trailed behind him more slowly, keeping his distance.

At the back of the building, Vinny was working silently, pulling at one of the pipes going into the air conditioning unit. He was still sweating, eyes moving to every noise, but his hands were steady. Abigale had left him to it, and the three of them were alone for now.

'Where are you planning on running the negotiations?' Ernie asked, glancing at Tyler.

Tyler exhaled slowly, glancing at the run-down walls of Gard Village—Senior Living. It was not an impressive sight with its old facings that were peeling, and walls that were well past needing a paint.

Ernie snorted, unable to decide which part of the idea amused him more. Vinny jumped, hitting his head on the air-con unit. He rubbed his head and didn't look at Ernie as he went back to working on the unit.

When Tyler said nothing, Ernie's mirth died. 'No. No one here knows about magic.'

'It has to be somewhere neutral.' Tyler was about to add more, but another voice interrupted him.

'Gentlemen, you must be parched with all this heat,' Betty said from the doorway. She was a thin, delicate woman that had the look of an aged porcelain doll, with curly grey hair that was thick despite her eighty-plus years. She held a glass of lemonade in one hand and a plate of biscuits in the other. 'Working in this heat must be making you so terribly thirsty.'

Behind her stood another half a dozen women, aged between seventy and ninety. It looked like Abigale had described the repairmen. All eyes locked onto the two Dragons with an almost predatory expression, various snacks and drinks that had been pilfered from the kitchen clutched in their arms.

Vinny turned just as the women reached him. He hesitated a second too long, and it gave them the chance to press in close and give him a glass. 'My dear, you look far too hot.'

'Here. You should drink this.'

'I could hold your tools?'

Vinny looked more like a deer in headlights than a predator should be allowed to.

Tyler watched the women with suspicion as a few eyed him, eyelashes fluttering slowly, and hips cocked to the side, including the ninety-year-old woman leaning on her walking frame. Of course, that might have been an issue with her hips, rather than deliberate.

'This is a retirement home, not a conference centre,' Ernie said quietly. Though he was beginning to feel he was in a bar or a dating show after the third wink was sent towards Tyler.

'I would not ask this if I had any choice,' Tyler said, turning to Ernie. 'There is nowhere else.'

'Nowhere else for what?' Betty asked, smiling as she handed Tyler a glass.

'We were due to have a reunion of sorts, but our venue had to cancel at the last minute,' Tyler said, accepting the glass and lying with the same smooth motion.

'A reunion?' Betty asked. Her eyes slid up and down Tyler's body as he took a sip of the lemonade. 'There are more of you?'

'Yes, my family is quite large,' Tyler said, smiling widely as he turned up his charm. 'This drink is lovely.'

'Betty—' Ernie started, but never got the chance to finish the warning as she talked over him.

'You should have it here. Once the air-con is fixed, of course. The communal living room is large. It could support quite a few people. We would be thrilled to entertain more of you.' Betty smiled. It looked innocent enough, but her eyes travelled across Tyler's arms. 'Any friend of Ernie's is welcome here. We hardly get any visitors.'

'You get plenty of visitors,' Ernie muttered. Betty ignored him.

'That is very generous of you, thank you. I don't know what I would have done.'

Betty smiled. 'Glad to help. Let me tell the ladies we will be having guests.'

Tyler watched Betty with a frown as she wrangled up the women. 'I didn't think they would agree so easily.'

Ernie did not say anything to that. If Tyler thought that a bunch of retired old ladies were going to be easy to deal with, then he was about to be educated. Betty had already made the offer, Ernie would have to play host. He smiled as he considered what Betty might do. 'I have conditions.'

'That is to be expected.' Tyler turned back to Ernie.

'All parties who come to the negotiation will agree to these terms before entering. I will not have my people put at risk.' Ernie considered his words before he continued, imagining the tension the two Alphas would bring. 'There will be no violence. Everyone here will be treated with respect and manners by all who step foot on the grounds. Most importantly, no one here knows that magic, or magic creatures like Dragons, exist. Your presence here will not alter that,' Ernie said, letting a thread of power weave through the agreement.

Tyler looked like he wanted to argue. But he nodded. 'Very well, I agree with your terms. I will send them to the Blue Flight.'

If the Dragons were going to make Ernie play the host, then they were going to get the full welcome that Gard Village—Senior Living could offer.

ERNIE HAD EXPECTED THERE to be some chaos while Betty brought round the staff to the idea of a reunion being held in the retirement home. But as it turned out, having men who looked like they could have walked off a fireman's calendar made everyone want to bend over backwards to assist. It also helped that Vinny had fixed the air-con, and the room was quickly growing cooler.

'It's wrong,' Jerry said, scratching at his bushy eyebrow as he took in the guests.

Well, almost everyone was happy.

'Men don't look like that. In my day, men had hair on their chests, and face. These are boys, hell…they're babies.'

Tyler and Vinny, plus two other Dragons, were currently clustered in a corner, surrounded by the majority of the women at the retirement home.

'How do you know they don't have hair on their chest?' Betty asked, pausing as she gathered more glasses. 'Of course, I can help you do a survey if you want. Just to be sure of your facts?'

She walked away before Jerry could finish spluttering. 'This is wrong. Just, wrong.'

'They are just here for the day,' Ernie said, watching as Betty stalked Vinny. He tried to evade and failed miserably. For a Dragon, he did not have very good hunting instincts.

'Why are you smiling?' Jerry was scowling at him again.

'I don't know what you're talking about,' Ernie said, wiping the smile from his face. Jerry stalked away, muttering to himself about hair and chests.

'The Blues have agreed to the terms,' Tyler said, moving to stand beside him, watching the group. 'You should remove the humans before they arrive.'

'This is their home. They have agreed to lend you their space. You cannot ask them to leave.' Ernie raised his eyebrow at the man. 'That wouldn't be very good manners.'

'This is Dragon business,' Tyler said, a thread of warning entering his voice. But he took one look at Ernie and moderated his tone. 'You said the residence could not find out about magic.'

'Then I'm sure you will find a way to be creative.'

'You're being unreasonable.'

'You agreed to the terms. They never stated privacy, nor should you have expected it. This is their home. Maybe you should have thought of that before you invited yourself.' Ernie turned to him, meeting his eyes. 'Unless you want to solve the war the other way, Tyler?'

'No.'

'Who is the Blue Alpha?' Ernie asked as Tyler ground his teeth.

'Lachlan Brightwing,' Tyler said, but he cut off before saying any more. A thread of angry heat pulsed through the room and every Dragon turned to the door.

The Blue Dragons entered with a loud clatter and a flash of sunlight as the doors burst open, banging against the walls. They moved as if nothing would stop them. Or they tried too.

Jerry chose that moment to cross the room, pace slower than was strictly necessary. The Blue Dragon's Alpha only just managed to pull himself up shortly before he hit Jerry.

'Careful, friend,' Jerry said, frowning at the group that was made up of four men. 'Wouldn't want you to hurt yourself.'

Lachlan was a middle-aged man with hair that had already gone silver. Age had done nothing to diminish his strength; his shoulders were wider than Tyler's. He stood with his back rigidly straight as he turned his icy blue eyes to Jerry. Another man would have stepped back. Jerry didn't have that kind of sense.

One of his men started to step forward like he intended to bodily remove Jerry. Ernie braced to interfere, but he never got the chance. All Lachlan did was turn to the man, and he froze mid-step. The presence of who and what the Alpha was rippled over the room, making Tyler's efforts feel like a tiny spark in comparison. Going by the singeing heat emanating from the man, he was very aware of that fact.

'You alright? You look a little pale?' Jerry might not have felt the magic, but he could see something was wrong. He stepped forward like he intended to support the stricken Dragon.

'My Son, Mason, will be fine. His lunch has disagreed with him, I believe,' the Alpha's voice was soft but no less powerful for it, and his words no less of a threat. Ernie could read between the lines easily enough.

'You here for the reunion too, then?' Jerry asked, frowning at the men.

The Alpha smiled, glancing at Tyler. 'Reunion. Yes. That is why I am here.'

THE TENSION BETWEEN THE two groups was so clear that even the humans exchanged glances. That no one questioned the tension said a whole lot about what their family reunions must have been like.

Betty, who was never one to let the awkward silence stop her from having a good time, stepped forward. 'Gentlemen, would any of you like a glass of lemonade?'

The pair of Blue Dragons behind Lachlan didn't quite know what to do as Betty thrust glasses into their hands. They looked at Lachlan with desperate eyes, but he ignored them as he watched Tyler.

'Betty—' Ernie started.

'You can help yourself, Ernie,' Betty said, not even glancing at him, as she turned and headed towards the Dragons who were trying their best to pretend the other group didn't exist.

Ernie scowled at her. That had not been what he was going to ask.

Mason, who still looked like he was shaking off the effects of his father's magic, tried to step away before Betty captured him as well, but Jerry got there first. Escaping wasn't going to be that easy.

'I wouldn't recommend the lemonade on an upset stomach. All that acid, no thank you. Ginger. That's what you need.' Jerry paused as Betty deliberately bumped into him as she passed with another pitcher. 'Of course, if your stomach was feeling fine, the lemonade is excellent. The best.'

Betty snorted as she ushered the two men towards the table that held snacks, and the other Gold Dragons.

Ernie had to admire her persistence. It wasn't every day you could get the two groups together without conflict, but with Betty standing there, they looked too frightened to do anything but drink their lemonade.

'I don't—' Mason started to speak.

'I have some ginger biscuits stashed. I'll be right back.' Jerry turned and headed in the direction of private rooms, moving at a relatively fast shuffle.

Mason stared after him. '—need any.'

Betty poured another glass and brought it over to Lachlan with a smile. He blinked at her, finally drawing his eyes from Tyler to accept the offering. She waited.

Ernie considered giving him a warning. Jerry hadn't been that far from the truth, the lemonade was not known for its soothing taste. In the end, Ernie decided he liked his peace and quiet more than he cared about Lachlan's discomfort.

Lachlan took a sip, managing a straight face, then smiled, giving her a nod. 'Thank you.'

Ernie was impressed. He could see the other Dragons wincing as they finally tasted their own lemonade.

Betty beamed. 'You're welcome. It's not often we get such... lovely... guests.' Betty managed to keep her eyes from wandering this time as she said it. She turned and moved back to the cluster to top up their full glasses.

'Lachlan,' Tyler said the name with cold precision, anger barely suppressed as he moved closer to the other man. Now that they were alone, he let some of that polite mask drop. 'You did not bring my Mate.'

Lachlan smiled; it did not come close to reaching his eyes. Mason moved forward a step closer to Lachlan, but he raised one hand.

'No,' Lachlan said, not even looking at Mason.

Mason shuddered, stepping away from his Alpha as though Ernie had not felt any power this time. Mason sent a glare towards Tyler, but he managed to stay silent.

'Her presence was not required.' His voice was low enough that it was lost in the general hum of conversation.

'She deserves a voice.' Tyler growled, eyes flashing amber as his power simmered. Ernie put one hand on his shoulder to stop him from doing something stupid. The rumble vibrated through Ernie's fingers.

Tyler exhaled slowly, visibly controlling his outward anger as the growl stopped. 'She made her choice. He cannot take that from her,' Tyler said, then he turned to stalk away towards the makeshift table Abigale had set up, not letting Lachlan reply.

Mason made a move to follow, but another gesture from Lachlan stopped him, a little less dramatically this time. Ernie was starting to like Mason less and less.

'The young today have no patience,' Lachlan said with a shake of his head like his words had made him sad. Ernie knew he wasn't. It was obvious in the way he allowed Mason to run.

'Patience is for when rewards are worth more than the pain. You expect much from the young without offering anything in return,' Ernie said, shaking his head as Lachlan blinked at him, obviously not expecting that answer.

'Who is this old man?' Mason said, eyeing Ernie from head to toe. He did not look impressed. The feeling was going around. 'How is he going to keep the peace when Tyler doesn't get what he wants?'

Ernie smiled at Mason, showing him wrinkles that were worn deep, and teeth that were stained. If that was all Mason could see, then he was more a fool than Ernie had thought.

'We are here to talk,' Lachlan said. His tone made it clear that this was not the first time he had said them. 'We will respect the neutral territory. So will Tyler.'

'Neutral.' Mason twisted his face as he looked Ernie directly in the eyes. To another Dragon, it would have been a challenge. 'They did not respect our territory. We should crush them.'

'Mason, you will show manners to our host. Do not make me warn you again,' Lachlan said, voice heavy.

Mason struggled against the command, because this time there had been power in them. Not the lash of power like the first time, but a slow burn. Mason fell back a step, head down.

'Ernie is our host, and his peace will be respected,' Lachlan said, eyes moving back to Tyler. 'We are all guests here.'

Mason flicked a sour glance at Ernie, like he doubted his father's words.

'I found them,' Jerry called, waving the biscuits as he shuffled into the room.

Mason took a step away, then visibly stopped himself from retreating further. 'You should send your people away, old man. This is Dragon business. The humans are not needed.'

'No.' Ernie watched Mason flush red; his oversized neck muscles twitched.

'This is their home,' Lachlan said, before Mason could make any more demands. It was almost amusing to watch the words stick in his throat. 'Asking them to leave would be considered rude.'

Ernie smiled at Lachlan, showing his teeth. The echo of Ernie's own earlier words was a surprise, considering what he had seen of the man so far. Ernie indicated to the mismatched tables and chairs that usually functioned as the poker table. 'Why don't we get started?'

Lachlan sent Ernie a look that could have meant anything from he was annoyed through to he thought it was funny. After a moment, he nodded. 'Very well, let's begin.'

Lachlan settled into the seat opposite Tyler. Their people managed to escape the group of older women and quickly moved to stand behind their Alphas. They left the glasses behind.

All except for Vinny, at least. He was stuck listening to Jerry talk about the benefits of ginger biscuits. Though, Ernie suspected the reason for Vinny's staying might have more to do with Abigale being there than Jerry. Going by the intent look Abigale was giving the biscuits, she was finding the conversation riveting.

It was a rather dull start. There was silence from both men. Neither willing to start. Ernie sat down between the two groups, leaned back so he could watch everyone.

'Tyler, why don't you start?' Ernie prompted. The day had already slipped into afternoon, and he had the feeling they would wait a lot longer without a push.

'My ma... wife should be here,' Tyler said, eyes flickering to Betty who passed by the table on her way to take Jerry's biscuits away. He did not look impressed.

'My sister is not his Mate,' Mason spat. The heat in the room rose with the tension.

'Wife,' Ernie corrected.

'She is not required,' Lachlan said tersely, with a side glance at his son.

'She made a choice,' Tyler said. 'Just because you do not agree, it doesn't give you the right to stop her.'

'This is not about my daughter,' Lachlan said, leaning forward. 'You broke the peace by entering my territory without my permission.'

'Mason kidnapped my Mate,' Tyler hissed.

'Wife,' Ernie said, watching Jerry try to convince Betty to give him back his biscuits. Vinny had taken the opportunity to try to strike up a conversation with Abigale.

Tyler gave Ernie an irritated look, then continued. 'I entered your home to make sure she was okay.'

'I rescued her from you,' Mason said, leaning forward on the table. He had kept his voice low, at least.

'Liar,' Tyler shouted, standing to slap his table. Every eye turned to him.

Ernie sighed as the silence spread until there was only the sound of breathing. They were never going to stop a war if this was their idea of communication.

'You all look like you could use a break. How about a game of poker?' Betty's voice cut through the tension. She drew and held every eye. Ernie couldn't decide if she just didn't sense the anger, or she was so used to dealing with a group of grumpy old men that she didn't care. 'Unless you're afraid of a lady beating you?'

Dragon pride was a dangerous thing. Even Vinny stepped forward at the challenge. Ernie didn't have the heart to tell them they were all going to lose.

Betty cheated.

BETTY SOMEHOW MANAGED TO relocate everyone around the table in what, at first, looked like a haphazard mix. But by the time she had finished, a Blue Dragon sat next to a Gold dragon with the old ladies seated between them. Jerry had managed to find a seat next to Lachlan.

Norris had squeezed into the space beside Betty, thankfully back to the socially acceptable clothing, which was to say he was wearing more than just his pants. He was not a small man, his belly large enough that he could sit back with his arms folded on top of it like a shelf.

Ernie had not so much decided to join the game, as he had been issued with his two cards and a firm look that dared him to argue. Abigale had been similarly pulled into the game, though the rest of the staff had managed to find a way to be busy elsewhere.

'We don't use real money here, gentlemen,' Betty said as she dished out an even number of worn chips. 'This way, everyone plays at an equal level.'

Betty sat back in her chair and drew the community cards face up on the table. Norris watched her like a hawk, still under the impression that if he watched her often enough, he could figure out how she cheated.

'So, what do you do for a living?' Jerry asked Lachlan, as the silence continued to hold.

Lachlan smiled, another one of those shark-like motions, all teeth and no soul. 'Construction. I find the process of building to be extremely rewarding.'

'You should spend more time building your foundations,' Tyler said, checking the cards in his hand.

Ernie rolled his eyes as he placed his own bet. The undercurrent was impossible to miss, but at least they were no longer talking about mates and territory.

'Foundations are important, but if you build without a plan, you are bound to fail.' Lachlan didn't even look at Tyler as he spoke.

Tyler pushed his chips in harder than was necessary. 'Yet inflexibility when planning will lead to problems that cannot be fixed.'

The temperature spiked, and the air-con kicked into higher gear, rattling as it tried to keep going. Norris started pulling at his collar like he was going to pull the button-up shirt open. Ernie kicked him under the table and sent him a warning look. No one needed to see that today.

Norris reluctantly lowered his hand. 'I wasn't going to take it off,' Norris muttered under his breath and tossed in his own chip.

'Never done much with construction,' Jerry said, cutting in before anyone else could speak. He smiled, but it was strained. 'Good money in it, I hear. Risks too.'

Lachlan waited for everyone to put in their bets before he spoke. The chips clicked together in the centre of the table. 'It's only risky if you don't know your market.'

'You make it sound dull,' Jerry said as Betty placed another community card face up. He checked his cards, tossing in another chip to match the bet. 'There is no fun without risk.'

'It's business, it's not meant to be fun.' Lachlan's voice was dismissive, but his head snapped round as Jerry snorted at him.

Ernie braced for Lachlan to overreact as the sound hung in the air. The rest of the table placed bets, or dropped out, but all eyes were on Jerry and Lachlan. Even Norris, who knew better, failed to watch Betty. They all missed her adjusting the cards in her hand.

'You disagree?'

Jerry waved at the table, including everyone. 'If it's not fun, why do it?' Jerry said, putting in his bet, letting Betty place the next card. 'What is the point?'

'To win.' Lachlan's smile was cold.

Those left in the game hurriedly placed their bets until it was only Jerry again. Ernie followed suit, sending a weak pulse of energy out as he did. Lachlan's eye twitched, but he gave no other signs of acknowledging the warning.

'What is the point of winning if you're not enjoying the game?' Jerry picked up his cards, checking them before he tossed another chip to match the bet.

Lachlan narrowed his eyes, energy rippling through the room, making the Dragons shiver. Jerry met the Alpha's eyes. Even though Jerry was only human, he couldn't have failed to feel the heat of them. Lachlan moved to throw in another chip impatiently, but Jerry put his hand over Lachlan's.

Ernie tensed, ready to react, and he was not the only one. Everyone looked ready to fight. Except Betty, who was scowling at Ernie like it was his fault, thought he had done nothing.

'You have thrown every chip in the centre without once looking at your own hand. You're playing blind, not even looking at the other players as you make your choice.' Jerry took his hand away, tapping his own cards. 'Loose or win, what's the point if you're not enjoying the game?'

'You talk about risk, but this game is pointless. There is no risk of losing, nothing gained if you win. What is there to enjoy without the risk too?'

'Then let's increase the stakes?' Jerry asked, raising one bushy eyebrow.

Lachlan looked at the cards, then straight at Tyler. 'There is only one prize here that matters.'

Tyler growled. 'I will not—'

'Unless you're afraid to lose?' Lachlan leaned forward, shoving away his cards he had never looked at once.

Ernie rolled his eyes. There was no way this was going to end well. 'No.'

Lachlan turned to him, smile tight. 'You wanted to assist us in negotiations. Your people talk about risk and reward. This seems like a good way to settle our problem. One game, the two of us. Winner takes all.'

'Three,' Betty said, pulling in all the cards. There was a small murmur of protest from the other women as they gave up their cards. 'Ernie should represent the house.'

'Betty, this is not a good idea.' Ernie leaned forward from his slouch, but she ignored him as she finished shuffling the pack and pushed out the cards. 'The stak—'

'Agreed.'

'Agreed.'

This time, it was Ernie who growled. Betty ignored him as she shoved two cards towards him. This was not going to end well.

ENERGY SIZZLED THE AIR around the table. Even the humans rubbed at the goosebumps on their arms.

Betty dealt all the cards rather than waiting for bets, since there was only one stake that mattered in this game. Ernie's cards lay face down in front of him; they were clear in his mind, but his fingers still twitched to check them.

Lachlan fingered his cards lazily, confident and pleased on the outside. In comparison, Tyler was anxious, fingers drumming the table as he watched Lachlan. Both were an act. Their energy sizzled in the air like static before a storm. Ernie didn't bother with a poker face.

Tyler would be the first to show his cards, but he hesitated to reveal them, eyes locked on Lachlan.

'Don't keep us waiting, boy,' Jerry said, rubbing his hands.

Tyler turned over his cards, showing a straight. The hand put him squarely middle of the road for a win.

Lachlan was next.

Ernie felt the energy shudder as Lachlan turned over his cards. The red flush was enough to beat Tyler's hand.

'Ernie?' Betty said, voice almost lost in the rumble coming from Tyler.

Ernie sighed and turned over his cards. The straight flush was more than enough to beat either hand.

The energy made the hair on his arms stand straight up as both men turned to Ernie.

'What the hell is this?' A woman's voice cut through the tension, redirecting it like a lightning rod. She was a petite young woman with black hair so dark humans would never notice the blue tint to it. Her bright, sea-blue eyes narrowed on the men.

'I am ensuring your future, Morag,' Lachlan didn't look at her.

'You were supposed to be—' Mason started to speak, but his sister talked over him.

'By playing games?' Morag looked at the table and three sets of cards. She frowned at the empty space where the chips should have been. 'What were you betting with, Father?'

Silence answered her. Lachlan and Tyler both turned to Ernie like this was somehow his fault.

Morag's eyes flashed, energy lashing out sharp enough to make all the Dragons wince. 'How dare you. You bet on me? Like I am a piece of property to be traded?'

'You were told that we would deal—'

Morag spun to Tyler, cutting Mason off. 'It doesn't surprise me that they would do something like this. But you. I thought better if you, Tyler,' Morag whispered, tears brimming in her eyes.

'It wasn't like that Morag. Please let me explain,' Tyler said, standing to rush around the table towards Morag. But almost as they had telepathy, the women in the room stood. Blocking his path.

'You bet on a woman?' Betty said, voice sharp as she took in all the hands, then her eyes landed on Ernie. 'I am disappointed in you, Ernie.'

'I did not—'

Betty moved to stand at Morag's side, patting her, drawing her away, ignoring Ernie entirely. 'Come, my dear, let's get you a cup of tea. I think the men need some time to reflect on what is appropriate.'

'—want to play this game.'

Another day it might have been amusing that Betty had somehow forgotten that the only reason he was involved in the bet was because of her insistence. Today, with eight sets of Dragon's eyes on him, he could not find the humour.

❦

'MORAG CAN'T DO THAT,' Mason said, narrowing his eyes at them, standing as if he intended to follow. 'She shouldn't even be here.'

'I wouldn't recommend it,' Jerry said, standing and straightening slowly, blocking Mason's path despite the size difference. Even human, he could have flattened Jerry.

'Mason,' Lachlan said, voice low with warning.

'No. I will not stand by while they take her away.' Mason's energy rippled. Ernie could almost see the scales under his skin. 'She doesn't know what she wants.'

'You will leave her alone.' Tyler stood and moved to stand beside Jerry. 'She made her choice, and if she never wants to see me again after my actions, that is her choice as well. I will not let you take any more of them from her.'

'Choice?' Mason shouted, stepping closer to Tyler. 'You have twisted her head so badly that she doesn't even know what she is choosing. I had to get her away from you.'

'You saw us together. You felt our connection. Are you so blind that you cannot admit that truth?' Tyler said.

'I did what I had to, so she would be safe. You're nothing but a jumped up—'

'Enough.' Lachlan stood, energy slamming out, knocking them both back a step. He turned to Mason. 'You told me she was being held against her will.'

'Never.' Tyler spat. 'Morag was free to come and go, happy. Until he came.'

'He was twisting her. She didn't know what she wanted.'

Tyler growled. 'She knew you would never accept the truth; she just had no idea you would go so far.'

'Get him out of my sight,' Lachlan said, voice quiet and low.

Mason smiled, turning to Tyler, but it didn't last long as one of the Blue Dragons grabbed his arm in a firm grip. He snarled, but the Alpha let the power flare to life again. Mason stumbled away with the guard.

Silence reigned as Tyler and Lachlan stared at each other.

Norris nudged Ernie on the side with his elbow. 'Just remember this moment the next time my family visits. This lot makes them look almost normal.'

Ernie snorted, shaking his head. It wasn't true, but he appreciated the effort. They were skirting the line of believability already without all the talk of mates. But in Ernie's experience, humans were generally quite happy to keep lying to themselves.

'My apologies for disturbing the peace, Ernie,' Lachlan said, voice formal.

Jerry snorted, interrupting before Ernie could reply. 'Disturbing the peace? You're going to be leaving in pieces if those women have their way. Betting your daughter; shame on you.' He turned to Ernie, raising an eyebrow. 'Does that mean she is your wife now?'

'No,' Ernie said quickly. Tyler's growl rumbled over the room.

'What the hell is that noise?' Jerry said, scratching at his ear. 'Vinny? Is the air-con still having problems?'

Vinny opened his mouth, then snapped it closed, glancing at Ernie 'Yes. System is still re-settling.'

'It's bloody annoying.' Jerry shook his head and stalked away, grumbling to himself.

THE WOMEN WEREN'T GONE long, not really, but it felt like a long time as the remaining Dragons sulked.

Betty preceded Morag's return. All eyes turned to her as she stood in the doorway, surveying the room. She glared at everyone in turn, then stepped aside so Morag could enter.

She looked at Lachlan in surprise when she noticed Mason was missing. But she didn't go to him.

'Why would you agree to something so stupid?' she said softly.

Tyler kept his eyes down as she approached him. 'I—'

'Actually, you know what? I know why.' Morag turned to her father with an angry glare. She muttered under her breath where the humans wouldn't hear it. 'Stupid Dragon Alpha's pride.'

'I would never have let them take your choice,' Tyler said, risking a glance at his Mate. She stood over him with an expression Ernie couldn't quite read. 'I never meant for it to get this far. Please forgive me. If you wanted to leave, I would under—'

She signed and pulled him close, kissing him before he could finish. She pulled back, both breathless. 'Of course, I forgive you, you silly oaf. But if I ever find out you tried anything this stupid—'

'Never,' Tyler said, wrapping his arms around her waist, smiling as he rested his forehead against hers. 'Never again.'

Lachlan watched them without expression. The energy in the room had changed as the two had come together. The clash and spark that had been like a raging river, directions randomly changing all afternoon, was now a still lake around the pair. Calm, strong, and settled. There was no missing the power of that bond.

They turned together to face Lachlan; hands clasped together. 'I have made my choice.'

'So it seems,' Lachlan said quietly.

The couple exchanged glances. 'Are you going to object?' Morag asked. Though she was trying to hide it, her nervousness was obvious. She did not want to go against her father, but she would.

'I was given incorrect information about the nature of your relationship,' Lachlan said. Jerry snorted loudly. 'You are not a child; I have no right to make your choices for you.'

'That is not an approval,' she said quietly, hand tightening on Tyler's.

Lachlan hesitated. 'Your Mate has proven to be willing to fight for you, and despite our poor choices this day, I find him acceptable.'

Tyler exhaled at the half compliment, but Morag squealed and rushed forward to hug her father. He stumbled back a step as she threw her arms around his neck. 'Thank you.'

THE SUN WAS CLOSE to setting by the time Ernie wrangled all the Dragons outside and on their way. The Blue's except for Lachlan had already left, presumably to manage Mason, who Ernie suspected was about to have a very bad day.

'Thank you for helping,' Tyler said, taking Ernie's hand in his, smiling at his Mate.

'Yes, thank you for stopping them from going to war,' Morag said, rolling her eyes. Tyler flushed, but she squeezed his hand to take the sting out of her words.

'I wish you luck with what comes next,' Ernie said, meaning it. They were going to need it. It wasn't often that the two different colours of Dragons became mates. There was a lot of history, a lot of distrust between the Flytes.

The rest of the gold Dragons followed them, except Vinny. He stood awkwardly with his tool bag in front of him like a shield once again. He shuffled his feet nervously as he spoke to Abigale. They said goodbye awkwardly,

Vinny almost falling over his own feet as he turned. Ernie winced as he watched them. A problem for another day.

As their energy faded, only Lachlan was left. Abigale sent them one last glance as she headed inside.

'Why would you risk your people like this?' Lachlan asked, pushing away from the wall of the house where he had been leaning to face Ernie. The ripple of energy was enough to level mountains. 'You could have said no to Tyler, not got involved.'

Ernie let the doors he kept closed against his power fall open. When he had put Tyler in his place that morning, he had barely turned the handle. Lachlan stumbled, falling to the ground, pale in the last of the day's light. Sweat beaded on his forehead as he kept his eyes down.

'Why would you risk yours?' Ernie said, closing the door tightly. Lachlan might have been able to level mountains, but Ernie could destroy planets. 'Don't expect me to believe that you were convinced by your son's lies. Tyler thought he was smart coming here. But he wouldn't have known what I was unless someone had told him. Or let him find out.'

'The world is changing, power shifting.' The words came out breathless as Lachlan forced himself to raise his eyes and meet Ernie's. The man's Dragon was almost visible under his skin, fighting against the motion. 'Then I hear a God is living on earth.'

Ernie exhaled slowly, damned rumours. He did not want people trying to find out who he was. He waited for the next question he knew was coming.

'Who are you?' Lachlan asked. The air tingled with the request.

'I have been known by many names,' Ernie said, wanting to not answer. But he had opened the door to the question. He crouched next to Lachlan and whispered the name in his ear. 'Freyr.'

'Why are you here?'

'I'm retired,' Ernie said. Lachlan blinked at him, waiting, as if expecting more. Ernie gave him nothing else as he stood and headed back inside. He might have to answer his name, but his choices were his own. And he didn't have to explain them to anyone.

The longest day of the year was done. Tomorrow had better be quieter. What was the point in being retired if everyone and their dog kept dropping in?

Flashes Of Ernie

Author's Notes

One of the writing communities I am part of often does a quarterly 'blog hop' where a bunch of indie authors publish a short under a thousand words story on their blog. They would then provide a link at the bottom to all the other authors who were taking part, allowing readers to hop between stories.

These Flashes of Ernie were all published for free on my blog between 2021 and 2022 (I believe) and I had a lot of fun trying to condense down Ernie's drama into a quick story.

From love, to winter, to WereRabbit's at Easter, I hope you enjoy this little collection of shorts.

A Ghost of a Trick, or Treat

THE DOORBELL CHIMED AGAIN, making Ernie shudder. Just a few more, then it would be over, he promised himself as he grabbed the bowl. One benefit of living at Gard Village—Senior Living was supposed to be that no one visited. No one had warned him Halloween was the exception.

Taking a deep breath, inhaling the lingering scent of burnt cookies that the staff had made, he opened the door. Two small children stared up at him.

'Trick or treat,' the tiny ghost child squealed loudly, like the volume might make up for the lack of height. Covered by a white sheet that brushed the ground, it was impossible to determine the exact age or gender. It held a plastic pumpkin tub thrust in front.

Seeing an easy win, Ernie grabbed a handful of sweets ready for a quick toss and a faster retreat.

'No, that's not how you do it, Max,' the little girl next to him said. She was a chubby-cheeked angel, fake white wings hanging lopsided. Her halo fell off her too small head, but she caught it and put it back up. 'You have to wait for them to answer.'

Ernie sagged, the bucket of sweets hanging loose in his hand. He had heard about as many jokes as he could take for this year's Halloween, but his turn manning the door was almost over. Why couldn't they just take the sweets and leave?

'He ain't dressed up. Mama said only those dressed up get the joke, Mazie,' Max said, but he didn't raise the pumpkin for the sweets again.

Ernie looked down at his old man visage; with his beige trousers, striped cardigan, and white polo shirt underneath. His glamour was far more authentic than theirs. He was especially proud of his eighty-year-old hands where they held the sweets basket. It was a far better glamour than either of them could imagine, and it suited him year round.

Mazie rolled her eyes, catching her halo as it toppled again. 'I'll show you how it's done. Trick or treat?' Mazie said, pushing forward her pumpkin in a replica of what the boy had done.

Ernie wasn't the only one to notice. 'Hey, that's the same as what I did!' Max said.

'Don't be a baby, Max,' Mazie said, nudging herself slightly in front. 'I'm in charge. Remember, mama said so.'

Little Max deflated, sniffling, and Ernie glimpsed blue eyes through two small holes in the ghost costume, tears brimming.

Ernie let the sweets in his hand fall back into the bucket. 'I think I'd like to see a trick,' he said.

The girl opened her mouth, taking a deep breath, but Ernie raised his hand and pointed at Max, who was still slumped in the ghost costume. 'From him,' Ernie added.

'He doesn't know any jokes. He's just a baby,' Mazie said, rolling her eyes, though Ernie doubted there was much difference in age between them.

'I'm sure he knows a trick,' Ernie said, crouching, so he was the same height as the boy.

Max shuffled his feet, head down. Ernie hated seeing him so sad, something that would be repeated at every house he visited, his sister taking the credit and putting him down. But it didn't have to be that way.

Ernie let his magic rise and solidify into an idea. It was glamour, much like the magic he used to build his own form. It coalesced, and he released it with a snap of his fingers towards Max.

The sheet fell to the floor at Max's feet. The little girl squeaked as she stared at her now translucent brother.

'Oh, I like that trick,' Ernie said, smiling as he filled the two plastic pumpkins that hung limp in both of their hands. 'Very good.'

'How did you do that?' Mazie asked, waving her hand through Max's arm. 'How did the sweets still go in the pumpkin?'

The boy looked at Ernie, eyes wide, hovering between fear and excitement. He smiled slowly as he saw how much his sister was getting frustrated. He raised his head high as he gave a small nod. 'I'm a ghost,' Max said, struggling to lift his full bucket.

'Show me how you did it?' Mazie said, stomping her foot, now ignoring Ernie.

Max shrugged. 'You're not a ghost,' he said, looking at the girl's halo.

This time it was Mazie who deflated. As she looked at their full buckets, she tucked a wayward sweet back inside that was threatening to overflow. It didn't take her long to do the maths as she looked between the buckets and Max.

'This is better than my joke,' Mazie said, voice hushed, a smile slowly rising on her face.

Ernie watched them leave with a satisfied feeling. It would only last a few hours, but with a trick like that, Mazie would have no choice but to include Max now. Ernie wasn't even worried that someone might find a ghost child odd. Humans were very good at ignoring what they couldn't understand. After all, it was Halloween.

As a bonus, he'd given away that last of the candy. Ernie headed back inside, handing the empty bowl to the next one in line to stand at the door.

Jerry looked at the empty bowl in his hands, a heavy brow rising. 'That many?'

Ernie smiled, shrugging noncommittally. No one said he had to give the sweets out fairly.

A VERY BONY CHRISTMAS

IT WAS THE MIDDLE of the night. Nothing was stirring, not even a mouse. Mostly because the volume of snoring coming out of Gard Village—Senior Living had been known to set off Earthquake warnings two towns away.

Ernie turned the page on his book, trying his best to block out the noise. Christmas eve was always hectic in the retirement home. Families who only came once or twice a year tried to cram time in their schedule for a flying visit, swarming the building with screaming children and squabbling teenagers, most left to run rampant.

Snoring aside, he was glad it had finally grown quiet.

Thump

Bang

Whoosh

The snoring continued like a backing track to the new and unwelcome noise. Most of the residents' hearing wasn't good enough for it to have woken them. The staff would be another matter.

Thud

Ernie slammed his book down beside him and got to his feet. So much for a quiet night.

The old building was worn down, and yellow with age, but much like its residence, it kept going, no matter what was thrown at it. In this case, as Ernie reached the communal living room, that something was a red stone fireplace, dust still settling around it.

The dust wasn't new. The fireplace, however, hadn't been there a few hours ago. Also new were the two feet dangling over the unlit fire. The woman in charge of the night shift was nowhere in sight. Hopefully, it would stay that way. Humans managed to rationalise the strangest things, but feet in the chimney might be a bit much.

A muffled voice cursed, then sneezed.

'Gesundheit,' Ernie said. The feet froze.

'Ernie?' Pierce's familiar voice asked cautiously.

'Were you expecting someone else?' Ernie said, fighting his smile as the feet wiggled helplessly. There were logs set up, ready for a fire to be lit under them. It was very tempting, but he resisted.

'Emm.. Well... You see...' Pierce waffled, voice muffled.

'Spit it out, Pierce. What are you doing?'

'It's Christmas!' Pierce said, making a polite noise as he slipped a little further, red pants now visible, if a bit soot stained.

'I noticed. It doesn't explain why there is a chimney in the living room,' Ernie said, moving closer, poking at the black boot.

'Hey! Don't touch,' Pierce said, squeaking as he slid a little further. 'Don't you dare pull—'

Ernie pulled on the boot.

A black cloud of soot whooshed through the room, choking Ernie, making his eyes water. The boot in his hand wiggled, making Ernie drop it with a jerk. The size nine landed with a thud and hopped around in a circle.

'I told you not to pull it,' Pierce said, coughing. His remaining leg and a part of a white bone hung in the fireplace.

The glamour that hid Pierce's true Draug form struggled to accommodate the lost foot, flicking like a blurry mirage, before it eventually collapsed all together. Without it, Pierces slid the rest of the way out of the chimney with a resounding thud. The red Santa suit hung off his frame like a blanket, smeared black with soot. He looked like a poorly thought out Christmas meets Halloween mash up.

'I could have got out on my own,' Pierce said, sulking as he clicked his fingers to try to get the attention of his wandering boot. He would have been a powdery white if not for the soot. His paper thin skin stretched over bone and sinew in a level of detail that was normally only seen in textbooks.

'You wouldn't have had to if you had used the door,' Ernie said, trying to sound grumpy, but the sight was too funny to capture any annoyance, despite the fact the boot was making for the exit. Ernie went after it, grabbing it before it got to the door and returned it to Pierce.

'I deserve a mince pie. And milk. And a carrot,' Pierce said, slamming his foot back where it belonged. 'Don't tell me you don't have it. It's traditional.'

'You're not Santa,' Ernie said, watching as the glamour fixed itself, the suit filling out in a quick gust of air, until a dirty, fat man, in a Santa outfit-down to the white beard-stood in front of Ernie. 'And no one here believes in Santa.'

'But I brought presents,' Pierce said, voice a high-pitched whine as he eyed the chimney. Ernie grabbed

Pierce's arm before he ended up stuck again. 'And I even wore the suit.'

There was such an earnest expression on Pierce's face that Ernie relented. After all, it was the human's Christmas, and there was all that stuff about giving. Ernie brushed dust off Pierce's shoulder and said, 'I have whisky and Christmas cake, but that's your lot.'

Pierce beamed, eyes lighting up. 'Even better, point me in the right direction.'

Ernie nodded towards the exit. The kitchen definitely had some whisky hidden away. He'd caught Jerry hiding it last week. As to the cake, well, half the families that came had brought some, and they had more than enough.

'Who made the chimney for you?' Ernie asked as they walked. Creating something like this wasn't in Pierce's power house.

'Oh,' Pierce looked over his shoulder at the red brick and shrugged. 'It came with the sleigh and suit.'

Ernie missed a step, pulling Pierce to a stop. 'Who's sleigh?' Ernie's stomach sank as he anticipated the answer.

'It's Santa's sleigh,' Pierce said, looking at Ernie like he was stupid.

'Don't you think he might need it?' Ernie said carefully. He'd not spent much time with the man, but some reputations preceded people, and this one generally didn't line up with the commercial, family friendly version of Christmas.

'Well, no, he's passed out at the Rabid Rabbit, and everyone knows you shouldn't drink and drive,' Pierce said, making a disgusted noise as he moved towards the exit. 'I thought I would borrow it for a bit.'

Ernie looked back at the chimney, wondering if anyone would notice its addition. It was a tough one, could go either way. Humans were weird like that.

Then he smiled. He'd never driven a magic sleigh before.

Were's the Rabid Rabbit

Ernie arrived as Pierce collapsed to the ground. His neck had been twisted 180 degrees, and the bones were trying to poke out from under the skin.

'Was that really necessary?' Pierce asked, head twitching as he tried to look across the room.

Ernie knew the man wasn't really dead, but even so, biology should have stopped Pierce talking when his head had been twisted 180 degrees. Maybe it was just wishful thinking on Ernie's part, but Pierce and silence had never been familiar.

Pierce had landed chest down on the floor. He was wearing what could only be described as a toga, but the too-thin material put him dangerously close to indecent. Apart from the broken neck, he otherwise appeared to be in good spirits.

'Did you start it?' Ernie asked, crossing his arms, and took in the man who had dropped Pierce. He was as large as a heavyweight wrestler and dressed in combat trousers and a black vest top. He would have stood out in a crowd without adding anything else, except for some reason he also had a thick coat of short white fur and two large floppy ears protruding from his head.

'You don't know that,' Pierce spluttered, flopping a little as he tried to roll towards Ernie.

'That wasn't a denial,' Ernie said, as he took in the rest of the bar.

The Rabid Rabbit was a small hole-in-the-wall bar that had seen better days. Its tables and chairs used to be battered wood that had seen one too many fights, but after a recent run in with some ghosts, that part had been upgraded.

The patrons were a mix of legends who had seen better days. All of them were watching Pierce with varying levels of disgust. The bar might have catered to the town's supernatural elements, but even they had their limits.

Ernie sighed as it became obvious that Pierce wasn't getting up on his own. Grabbing him under the armpits, Ernie dragged him upright. Ernie's eighty-year-old body wouldn't have had the leverage, or strength, to lift Pierce's taller form if he'd been human, but since they were in a bar that catered to everything but humans, Ernie was sure no one would care that he was breaking the rules.

Now that Pierce was upright, the twisted neck looked so much worse. His glamour was slowly failing as it struggled to make him look normal and failed. His skin paled and his hair turned bone white. He blinked, eyes glowing bright red. The smell of old death rose around them, not the scent of rot, but of bone dust and wet dirt in an old crypt.

Ernie waited for Pierce to steady his balance, then reached up, putting a hand on either side of Pierce's face as he twisted.

Someone vomited loudly at the back of the room. It was violent enough to be heard over the snap of bone being forced back into place. Ernie held Pierce's head until he could feel the muscle under the skin writhing back into place. Being undead had its benefits. Today that included not having a real nervous system, meaning no pain.

'Thanks, Mate,' Pierce said, rolling his neck as it finished healing. His glamour settled back around him, skin moving back to a human pale, and hair turning white blond. His eyes lingered red, the colour toning down slowly until most people would assume they were brown.

'What the hell are you?' the furry man asked.

Ernie looked at Pierce, who was studying his fingernail with an intent focus. 'Can't you pick on people your own size, Pierce?' Ernie asked. 'You're a Draug, not an Ogre.'

Pierce snorted. 'There is no one his size.'

'Draug are monsters from legend, fierce undead creatures that rip apart people who try to steal their treasure,' the furry man said. 'You couldn't strike fear into a coward.'

'What do you know, you're the Easter Bunny,' Pierce said snidely, flicking his hair out of his eyes as he turned his back to the man. 'Stereotypes like that are what is wrong with this world.'

Ernie stepped forward, pressing a pulse of power out in warning before the man-rabbit could do more than snarl. Ernie was starting to see how Pierce had got his neck broken the first time.

'I am not the Easter Bunny.' The man sounded more wolf than human or rabbit. 'I am a WereRabbit.'

There was silence in the room. It was quite impressive really how solid it was. Pierce, of course, had to be the one who broke it as his snigger broke free. Ernie wished that kicking Pierce would make him shut up, then considered doing it just to make himself feel better. But he didn't get the chance as the WereRabbit came at Pierce.

Ernie caught the WereRabbit's fist that had been aimed at Pierce's jaw. The WereRabbit tried to kick instead, so Ernie twisted. Bone snapped. Unlike Pierce, the WereRabbit could feel pain. The scream made Ernie wince.

The WereRabbit fell to his knees, putting him closer to Ernie's height, so Ernie put him to sleep with a quick Glasgow kiss. The WereRabbit hit the floor with a thump.

The room was silent as Ernie took in each of them. 'Who the hell is turning Werewolves into WereRabbits for Easter?'

A slip of a woman started towards the back exit, but one of the other patrons grabbed her arm and pulled her out in front of the room. The woman flushed red. 'It was just a joke.' Ernie continued to stare at her as she shuffled her feet. 'For April Fools,' she added.

'Fix it,' Ernie said, then when she opened her mouth to speak again, he added, 'Now.'

The woman pouted but pulled her arm free of the person holding her to go to the Werewolf on the floor.

'Told you it was worth coming down for a drink today,' Pierce said, smiling as he slapped Ernie on the back. 'Happy April Fools.'

'I don't think you're quite understanding what that means,' Ernie said, but Pierce ignored him as he waved to the bartender. Ernie really needed to stop answering Pierce's calls.

A Touch of Summer Fire

THE FIRE BLAZED WITH golds and yellows, reaching outward, lighting up the entire yard despite the dark sky above. No one who passed would be too concerned that it might spread as the grass under it turned brown. Gard Village—Senior Living's garden had suffered worse discolouration during the drought season.

Unfortunately, the man inside the fire was another matter, and not so easy to ignore.

He stood hunched, unburned, and naked under the flames that licked his skin, with his hands cupped around his crotch in an attempt at decency.

'Do you mind doing this somewhere else?' Ernie asked, scowling. After all, what was the point in wearing the form of an eighty-year-old if you couldn't be grumpy? He even had good reason for a change. Being woken in the middle of the night by the sound of crackling fire had not been on his night-time plans.

'Are you Ernie?' the man asked, eyes a fraction too wide.

'Who's asking?' Ernie asked, scowl etching deeper. The man felt mortal. Humans were not prone to being writhed in a living flame.

The man hesitated, frowning at Ernie as if he were the odd one out. 'Bob.' The lie was a little too quick. 'I need your help.'

Ernie looked over his shoulder at the ugly squat building that was his home. No one had come to investigate the fire yet, a small blessing in a retirement home where more people seemed to sleep during the day than at night. He needed to sort this mess out before someone became curious. 'Just put it out.'

'If it was that easy, don't you think I would have done it?' Bob said, freeing one hand so he could shake it. One small ember leapt free and set a small patch of grass on fire. 'It won't go out.'

'How do you normally put a fire out?' Ernie asked, rolling his eyes as he stamped out the baby ember. It hissed in protest as it died. The summer heat had already been bad enough, but with the extra warmth from the flames, it was getting oppressive.

'Normally?' Bob's voice hit a painful note. 'There is nothing normal about this.'

Ernie sighed. Maybe he was asking the wrong questions. 'What happened?'

'Well. You see. I didn't really mean it.' The flames glowed hotter, as if reacting to his embarrassment. 'It was a joke. Everyone likes a joke, right?'

Clearly, they didn't, but Ernie didn't state the obvious.

'Look, mate, please. You gotta help me. My wife will kill me if I go home like this,' Bob said, taking a small step forward. 'He said you could fix it.'

'Who?' Ernie knew he probably wouldn't like the answer. Bob's hesitation solidified that belief.

'He was there when the guy did the thing with the fire. Stringy fellow, with a multi-headed skeleton dog.' Bob tried to sound casual, but Ernie heard the hitch in his voice. The fire crackled, like it wanted to add to the story. Ernie ignored it.

'Pierce?' Ernie asked, voice coming out in a growl. How the hell did one Draug cause so many problems? 'He told you to come here?'

'Yeah, we were partying across town at a place called the Rabbit something?' Bob got a faraway look, somewhere between horror and awe. Ernie had seen the look before.

'The Rabid Rabbit?' Like there was anywhere else it could be. It was the only place in town that catered to supernaturals. Normally they didn't allow humans inside, but apparently, someone had got bored.

'Yeah, that's it,' Bob said, almost letting go of his modesty before he caught himself. 'It was something else.'

Ernie stayed silent, trying to imagine how a naked man on fire made it through the city with no one noticing. 'You walked all the way across town, over the bridge that spans the river, and it never occurred to you to just take a dip?'

The man stared at Ernie, mouth hanging open.

Ernie rolled his eyes, turning back to Gard Village.

'You can help me, right?' Bob sounded desperate, fear breaking through his bravado. The fire made a little high-pitched popping sound, growing hotter.

Shaking his head, Ernie turned on the tap that was connected to the sprinklers. Water sprung up in several arcs over the garden.

The man yelped as the water hit him, making the fire hiss and curse. Several pieces leapt for safety, but the water was too widespread. Slowly, the fire grew smaller, until there was nothing but the smell of wet earth.

'It was that easy?' Bob said, staring down at his wet naked body. 'Just add water?'

'It's fire. What did you think would put it out?' Ernie said, keeping clear of the spray.

Bob blushed. 'Well. I should probably go now. Thank you. I think.'

'Don't go back to the bar,' Ernie said, wincing as the man turned to show him a second moon.

Bob made a noncommittal sound as he headed out of the garden.

Humans. Sometimes Ernie wondered how they had lasted this long. He hoped the man would wake in the morning thinking it had all been an odd dream, but really, it wasn't up to Ernie to sort it out.

With a rising sense of suspicion, Ernie checked his phone to find a message waiting for him.

'Sent you a present. Wish you were here, Pierce.'

Ernie rolled his eyes and kept scrolling down. There was a photo along with the message. Pierce posed beside an Ifrit, shot glasses raised, an all too familiar bar behind them. At least that explained the living flame.

Ernie sighed, glancing at the clock. It wasn't like he was going back to sleep now. The pair needed someone to keep an eye on them.

That was the only reason he went out. To keep them in line.

I Dream of a Snowman

THE LONG STRETCH OF water running from the front door towards the kitchen was the first sign something was wrong.

There wasn't any need for a second one. But just in case the horror-movie-worthy trail wasn't enough on its own, the front door to Gard Village—Senior Living banged against the wall, bringing a flurry of sleet inside.

Ernie heaved a sigh. Not another one.

He caught the door before it could bang a second time and checked outside. Green grass peeked through a white landscape of fast melting snow. There was no sign of anything out of the ordinary. He closed the door, making sure it caught properly, and turned to follow the trail to the kitchen.

'This one won't be as bad,' he whispered. But he already knew he was lying to himself before he entered the kitchen.

A five-foot-tall snowman stood in front of the freezer; a box of ice-cream balanced in his makeshift stick arms. Its body had been made from two large balls of snow, with a much smaller ball for its head. It had traditional pebble eyes and a carrot nose, which, after what had been used to make the last one, was a relief.

As soon as it saw Ernie, it tried to freeze in place, but it was too little too late. If Ernie had been anything remotely human, there would have been no explaining this one away.

'Relax, I'm not a mortal,' Ernie said, stepping over the water trail to move closer.

'Thank goodness,' the snowman said as he sagged. The ice-cream slipped from his twig hands. There was a moment of scrambling, where he almost caught the box, then it clattered to the floor, the plastic smashing. 'Sorry.'

'Why are you here?' Ernie asked, watching the snowman try to shovel part of what might have been his hip into the freezer.

The row of pebbles that made up the snowman's mouth curved into a smile. 'Well, when two snowballs really like each other, it makes—'

'No,' Ernie said, cutting in before it could finish the sentence. He'd already heard the joke once too many times this winter. 'I mean, why are you here? In my kitchen. You should be outside.'

'Oh,' the snowman said, clearly disappointed he didn't get to explain. 'I mean, surely it's not every day that you find a living snowman in your kitchen? I would have thought how I was made might have been more interesting?'

Ernie stared at the snowman as a large chunk of snow fell off one shoulder. His smile was gone now, and he slumped forward, not just because of the missing snow.

'Alright, tell me how you were made,' Ernie said, pressing two fingers to his head. Who knew Gods could get headaches?

'I don't want to anymore. I don't need your pity,' the snowman said, voice taking on a distinctive whine more appropriate for a five-year-old. An echo of the child who made it slipping in, a shadow of their imagination and life. And like a shadow, it was just as fleeting.

Ernie shook his head, not wanting to dwell on that thought. Stopping the snowman from melting in his kitchen was definitely a higher priority. Ernie didn't want to clean up all that water. Unfortunately, the freezer wasn't doing much to keep the snowman together. There was just too much heat, indoors and outside.

'No. Really, I want to know,' Ernie said, offering the snowman a smile. If he could get the thing outside, this would go easier. 'None of the others told it as well.'

'Others?' the snowman said, growing more sullen. 'There are others?'

'None as...' Ernie said, grasping for a word to describe three balls of snow, '...good looking as you.'

'You're just saying that because you feel bad,' the snowman said, head tilting precariously forward as he wrung his bark-covered hands together.

'No, no,' Ernie said, panicking as the pebbles around the snowman's eyes grew watery. 'The last one was just one big ball. You are much more impressive.' Politer too. The last one had thrown a tantrum, soaking the kitchen.

'It takes skill to make us, you know, real skill. Not everyone can do it,' the snowman said, straightening. He had to grab for his nose as the carrot came loose. 'My maker was excellent. I mean, look at my buttons! They are almost all the same size.'

Ernie watched one of the shiny glass beads the snowman was pointing to slide free with a chunk of snow. If he didn't get the snowman outside soon, there was going to be nothing left to save. Not that he would survive much longer outside with the warming weather.

'Oh, dear.' The snowman stared at the pebble. 'That's not a good sign.'

It was frustrating watching the realisation come to the snowman that something was wrong. It was the third one this week, and with the snow outside almost gone, it was likely going to be the last. Ernie had never seen so many snowmen drawn here in all the years he'd been pretending to be mortal.

'Why are you here?' Ernie asked gently, trying again to find out what was drawing them here.

'This place felt different. I thought maybe there would be something here to help. I felt safe, I think. Some kind of magic,' the snowman said, staring at Ernie. 'But it's not enough, is it?'

'No,' Ernie said, wincing. His magic was drawing them? But why now? His magic was of summer, not winter.

'But I made him happy while I was here, didn't I?' the snowman said. 'My maker I mean?'

'Of course you did. Why else would he have made such an excellent snowman?' Ernie said, closing the distance to pat its shoulder, careful not to dislodge any more snow.

'Will he remember me, you think?'

'Yes,' Ernie said, swallowing hard as the magic holding the snowman together started to collapse. This wasn't his magic, Ernie reminded himself. He shouldn't interfere. 'Every time the snow falls, he will remember.'

'Thank you,' the snowman breathed. Another lump of snow fell free, but this was one fragment too many and the lower half could no longer support the top. Snow crumpled on itself as it lost its shape.

Another life gone.

Taking a sharp breath, Ernie's patience snapped, and he grabbed the loose threads of the magic and held them. He was tired of watching them fall apart. The mess aside, it wasn't fair. They deserved to exist longer than the cycle of the weather. But that was how the magic of children worked, fleeting wisps of dreams.

With a slow breath, he put a piece of his will into the weave of the magic and whispered, 'every time they dream of a snowman, they will see you.'

The magic whipped away from him, silent and swift as it caught the tail edge of winter's air. It probably would not stop future snowmen visiting, but this one would get a chance to live on in the hearts and minds of children who made the next one.

That had to be enough.

LOVE, DRUNK AND CUPID

THE HIGH-PITCHED BEEP WAS enough to drive Ernie to violence. He followed it, forcing himself to take slow, calm steps as he entered the kitchen.

He wasn't sure what he had expected to find, but it certainly wasn't a naked man slumped half inside the fridge.

The man was almost six feet tall, with dark hair, and blue, somewhat bleary-eyes. His knee was bent, preserving a small portion of his dignity. At Gard Village—Senior Living, finding a naked man roaming around the place wasn't entirely unheard of. But they were never young, and never had large, white wings sprouting out their back.

'Can I help you?' Ernie asked, crossing his arms to glare at the man as the fridge beeped again.

The man blinked rapidly, as if he couldn't quite bring Ernie into focus. He waved a bottle of milk in Ernie's direction, then slurred. 'Who're you?'

'Since this is my house, how about you answer my question first?' Ernie considered slamming the fridge shut as it beeped again, but the man's wing twitched where it was caught in the door.

'Not yours.' The man sniggered, taking a swig from the bottle. It had a suspicious yellow tint. 'Retirement Home.'

'You're drunk.' Ernie snatched the bottle out of the man's hands as he moved to take another swig. The sickly sweet smell was overwhelming. No wonder he was drunk.

The man tried to catch it, but the fridge proved to be too complicated of a trap for his milk and honey addled brain. He grunted. 'Not drunk.'

Ernie rolled his eyes, choosing to ignore the obvious lie. 'Are you not supposed to be working?'

The man's eyes filled with tears, and he slumped back. 'Fired.'

Ernie looked at the man's wings again. They were intact, despite what looked like honey sticking the feathers together. 'What happened?'

The man sniffed loudly and dragged a broken bow up off the floor beside him. The wood was burned into two pieces, the string the only thing keeping it together. It was barely big enough to fit in the man's hand.

The magic that made all Cupids quick, small, and agile was in their bow. Without it, they were effectively barely more than humans with wings, glamour and really good matchmaker skills. If the bow was broken, that would explain the full sized man shape, but not why he was in Ernie's kitchen and still had his wings.

'I was the best.' Cupid shook his head. Blinking away the tears. 'I didn't know what she was. If I'd known, I'd not have shot her.'

'Who did you shoot?' Ernie chose his words carefully, trying to sound polite.

'Freya,' Cupid said, growling the word. 'She made them sack me, called me incompetent.'

Ernie winced. That sounded like his sister all right. But Cupid was still missing something out. 'And they left you with wings?'

Cupid looked away, not answering, both wings twitching. The wings were what made Cupid Immortal. To lose them as well as his bow would truly make him only human.

Ernie narrowed his eyes. 'Tell me you didn't run?'

'I didn't run,' Cupid said, wincing as he glanced at Ernie. He was starting to sound like he was sobering up. 'I hid.'

Ernie rolled his eyes. Of course he had. Why else would he be sitting in Ernie's retirement home kitchen, in a town in the middle of nowhere? 'And you didn't think I'd notice?'

Cupid gave a weak smile, tried to lean forward, but his wing got stuck. He blinked at it as if only just noticing it was wedged in the door.

'You should probably hide your wings. Mortals get a bit excited about that kind of thing,' Ernie suggested with a sigh. 'Then once you're sober, maybe you can tell me the rest of the story.'

CUPID WAS ABLE TO hide the wings with glamour after the third attempt, though Ernie was sure the fridge was never going to close properly again after the dent. But it had at least stopped beeping. He had even found some clothes for Cupid. The trousers came up to his mid calves, and the shirt didn't close, but it was covering the important parts.

'My head,' Cupid groaned, holding his head in his hands as he leaned on the worktop.

'Stop whining, you chose to drink,' Ernie said, hiding his smile as Cupid grumbled.

'What now?' Cupid asked, looking at Ernie with fear. 'You going to call Freya?'

Cupid was not stupid; Freya had a reputation as a huntress. She wasn't going to let someone hiding stop her hunt. She would want to make sure Cupid was mortal.

Ernie considered him for a moment, then sighed. 'Hell no.'

He slapped Cupid on the back. A deep power vibrated through Ernie's fingers as he cast magic out over Cupid in a kind of net. It would wear down over time, but it would give him a few years to stay hidden. After that, Cupid would have to find his own way to hide. That would drive his sister up the wall.

Cupid stared at him in surprise. He knew enough about magic to know what Ernie had done. He exhaled slowly, nodding his head. 'Thank you.'

'You'll need a new name,' Ernie said, turning away. Cupid was going to need a lot more than that if he wanted to survive in the human world. But a name was a good start.

He looked down at the broken, singed wood that used to be his bow. 'Archer?'

'As good as any,' Ernie said with a shrug.

'Thank you, Freyr,' Archer said, using Ernie's true name as he offered his hand. 'I don't know how to repay you.'

'If Freya finds you, tell her I helped hide you,' Ernie said immediately, enjoying the image of his sister having that tantrum. Hopefully, after quite a few years.

'Let me know if there is ever anything else I can do to return the favour,' Archer said, smiling as he pushed back from the counter.

Archer left the bow on the floor as he walked out of Gard Village—Senior Living to start his new life.

Ernie felt his sisters' presence tickle against his skin a few moments later. She practically walked past Archer and never even saw him. Ernie smiled. Her frustration stained the air. This was going to be fun.

RABID RABBIT'S REVENGE

NIGHT HAD SETTLED AROUND Gard Village—Senior Living, leaving the building dark and quiet. Or as quiet as a home with thin walls, and old men who could win contests in snoring ever got.

It was one of the few times that Ernie could sit and read his book uninterrupted, without anyone—

Tap. Tap. Tap.

The sound came from his window, faint under the chain-saw-like drone of the snores. But Ernie didn't care enough to go check.

He was reading his book and no one was—

Tap. Tap. Tap. The rattle on the glass came again. 'Pisst. I'm looking for Ernie?'

Ernie scowled at the curtain. The smell of wet fur seeped into the room. Did no one respect the privacy of sleep any more? Not that Ernie needed sleep, of course, but still, it was—

Tap. Tap. Tap.

'What—' Ernie hissed as he crossed the room to shove open the curtains. The rest of the words shrivelled up as he took in the... Ernie struggled to give it a name as the creature stood frozen in the light from the window, eyes wide like it was about to bolt.

It stood as tall and straight as a man, with white fur, long floppy ears, a small pink nose, and tiny whiskers that stuck out from each side of its face. At least Ernie knew where the wet fur smell had come from. The creature was soaked through from the spring drizzle. Though that was the least of Ernie's concern.

'Umm,' it said, taking another step back, so it was half in the shadows. 'Hi. I'm Bob.'

'What do you want?' Ernie said at last, lifting the window. Even for him, a WereRabbit outside his window was strange.

'You have to help!' Bob said, hoping a step closer. 'Everyone is affected.'

Ernie blinked at it slowly, waiting for more information, but nothing else was provided. It just continued to watch Ernie with its far too enormous eyes.

'Who is affected? By what?' Ernie asked after an uncomfortable moment of silence.

'The Rabid Rabbit! Everyone has changed. You have to come fix it!'

'Who told you I could fix...' Ernie trailed off, giving the damp WereRabbit another once over. Only one person would send something like this out in public. 'Pierce?'

Bob nodded his head rapidly, taking another hop closer with his excitement. 'Pierce said you could fix it!'

Of course he had.

'And what am I meant to do, exactly?'

Bob's face fell, tears hovered on the edge of falling.

'Alright!' Ernie said hurriedly before there were full on waterworks. 'I'll help.'

'Thank you!' Bob said, bouncing on the balls of his feet, like he was ready to dart away that second.

'Wait there,' Ernie said with a sigh as he closed the window. He needed to find Pierce a hobby.

THE RABID RABBIT WAS a small hole-in-the-wall bar in the centre of town. It was the only non-human bar in the area, and it made the best use of the rather dubious honour.

Ernie stopped in the doorway as he entered. A rather potent scent crawled up Ernie's nose, making his eyes water. Ernie didn't look too closely at the floor. The place was filled with... Rabbits. Not all had a human form like Bob, but none of them were the size that a rabbit should have been.

In the centre of it all, one man sat at a table alone. Entirely human in looks and apparently unaffected by whatever magic had spread through the bar. He had a small smile on his face as he watched the chaos. There was something familiar about him.

The smile slipped as he caught sight of Ernie, but he didn't make a move to leave.

'Ernie!' Pierce's voice came from the mouth of a grey rabbit near the scarred wooden bar. He was drinking a very orange coloured liquid. 'You made it!'

'What are you doing, Pierce?' Ernie said, crossing his arms as he watched Pierce down the rest of his drink. 'Transformation magic doesn't affect you.' Because that was what it was, Ernie was certain. Though the why escaped him.

'I was feeling left out,' Pierce said, smiling, showing two giant bunny teeth.

Ernie shivered and looked away. Pierce had done a good job replicating the image, but that smile just wasn't natural. Ernie would have preferred to see Pierce's Draug form. When a skeleton looked better, that said a lot.

'Why didn't you just call me on the phone?' Ernie asked.

'And what would the fun in that be?' Pierce said, whiskers twitching.

Bob scowled at Pierce. Or at least Ernie thought it was a scowl. It was difficult to tell under the fur. 'You said I had to go in person. What if a human believed I was a WereRabbit?'

'Don't be such a worrywart. No one would ever have been able to prove it on April Fool's day,' Pierce said, laughing as he slapped the man on his fur covered back.

Ernie rolled his eyes as he grabbed the angry WereRabbit by his arm.

'Tell me what happened?' Ernie asked, deciding to distract Bob before things turned nasty.

'Him!' Bob said, pointing to the human shaped man in the centre of the room.

'The Werewolf?' Ernie asked, eying up the man. This magic wasn't something Shifters could usually do. They could only change themselves, and usually only into one animal. But Ernie had finally remembered where he'd seen the man before. Last April, the Werewolf had been changed into a WereRabbit, a lot like Bob.

'Does he look familiar to you?' Pierce said, scooting back over the bar to accept another glass of orange liquid that the bartender gave him.

'Turn them back,' Ernie said, shaking his head. The bar grew quiet as they watched the exchange, waiting to see what was going to happen.

The Werewolf scowled at Pierce. 'They deserved it.'

'I'm sure I've seen him somewhere before?' Pierce said, squinting at the man as he nudged Ernie.

'Maybe if I spun your head around the other way, it would jog your memory?' the Werewolf said.

'You could try. Though I don't know how it would help. I wouldn't be able to see you anymore?'

Ernie rolled his eyes, elbowing Pierce in the side to shut him up. 'I don't care if they deserved it. Turn them back now,' Ernie said.

'Why should I? They enjoyed this joke so much last year, after all?'

'Last year, I didn't have rabbit shit all over my floor,' the bartender piped up. He had also taken on the shape of a rabbit, though a suspiciously petite one that allowed him to fit behind the bar. There was a lot of silence, and people shuffling their feet to that declaration.

Pierce tapped his finger on his lips. 'You were at the Christmas party, right? That's where I know you from?'

The Werewolf snarled and pushed to his feet.

'Think carefully about how this ended for you last time,' Ernie said, crossing his arms. He might not have looked impressive in his old man form, but the Werewolf remembered Ernie well enough. Last time he'd taken a swing, Ernie had broken his wrist.

The Werewolf turned away.

'Good choice,' Ernie said. 'Now turn them back.'

'The curse will wear off at dawn,' the Werewolf muttered.

All but Bob cheered, making the Werewolf jump.

'This is awesome!'

'Best April Fools EVER,' one of them said.

The Werewolf looked taken aback as another slapped him on the back. 'This is great. Way better than last year.'

'Great? How is this great?' Bob said, scowling. 'My wife will kill me if I drag fur over her house.'

'Sounds like a great excuse to keep drinking to me,' Pierce said, taking another swig of his drink. Someone had refilled it.

The bar patrons cheered again, calling for a round of drinks, pulling Bob and the Werewolf deeper into the chaos. They seemed confused, but pleased to be dragged into the group of very happy rabbits.

'Are you going to buy me one of those?' Ernie said to Pierce, giving him a sideways look.

'Only if you tell me where I know him from,' Pierce said, voice holding a whiny pitch. 'It's really annoying me.'

Ernie rolled his eyes.

'What do you remember about last April Fools?' Ernie said, smiling as he slapped Pierce's shoulder. This was going to be fun.

HIGHLAND RIFT PACK SERIES

Buried by Earth

Book 1 of the Highland Rift Pack Series

Sam has spent the last decade hiding her magic. If anyone found out she was an Earth Elemental, she would lose everything, including the land that relied on her.

Hale has been the Highland Rift Pack

Alpha for the last seven years, and his priorities are his pack, the rangers, and keeping the Highland Rift Scar monsters in check.

When a full moon hunt ends with Hale stung by a Rift scorpion and stuck as a wolf, Sam is forced to allow him to stay on her land. Something her land is ecstatic about. Her, not so much.

Though she tries to avoid him, it's not long before another attack puts Hale's life in the balance. Sam is left with a difficult decision: keep her secret and lose Hale, or risk everything and use her magic to save him.

Can Sam and Hale trust each other, or will their mistrust bury them? Find out in this enthralling paranormal romance novel, Buried by Earth, the first in the Highland Rift Pack series.

https://jemmaweir.com/books/highland-rift-pack/buried-by-earth/

—ℓℓ—

Bitten By Frost

Book 2 of the Highland Rift Pack Series

Amelia's Pack sent her north as a punishment for rejecting the Alpha's son as her mate. But for the first time, she feels free. Now, she's never going to let anyone close, not even the frustrating scientist who's testing her patience and self-control.

For years, Mitchel has hidden his Frost magic, protecting his family's reputation. But when he goes north to investigate why the Highland Rift Scar has shrunk, the cold is making his magic slip. Or maybe it's just the stubborn Shifter who is assigned as his escort.

As an investigation turns into a rescue mission, Amelia is left injured, and Mitchel on the edge of losing control of his magic. To give them a chance to heal, the Alpha benches the pair, but it's not long before more trouble arises, and only the two of them are left to help.

When Mitchel has already lost control once, and Amelia can barely stand, will they be able to learn to work together? Or will this new threat tear them apart?

Filled with suspense and romance, Bitten by Frost is a thrilling paranormal romance that will keep you on the edge of your seat. If you enjoyed the first book in the series, Buried by Earth, you'll be sure to love what this book offers.

https://jemmaweir.com/books/highland-rift-pack/bitten-by-frost/

Battered by Storms

Book 3 of the Highland Rift Pack Series

Staci's storm magic has always set her apart from the rest of the town, but she's always had her mum. Until now. With her mother's mind and health in decline, Staci faces the prospect of a life of isolation.

Oliver's family has always told him that he'll never amount to anything, but now he's an Alpha with a pack of his own. But not for long. At the end of his year at the Highland Rift Scar, he must give them both up, even if he has more than one reason to stay.

When a dangerous storm hits the town, Staci's magic fails her, and only Oliver can protect her from the destructive force trying to drain her magic. As the storm finally dissipates, Staci is blamed for the storm's creation, and Oliver is faced with an impossible choice that could put everyone he loves in danger.

Can Oliver find a way to keep Staci safe and protect his pack, or will forces beyond their control tear them apart?

Join Staci and Oliver in this thrilling paranormal romance novel as they weather the storm and find a way to be together. Will they be able to withstand the storm and find a way to be together, or will they be torn apart forever? Find out in the third book of the Highland Rift Pack Paranormal Romance Series.

https://jemmaweir.com/books/highland-rift-pack/battered-by-storms/

WISHING FOR TRUTHS

Contemporary Fantasy Short Story

Vanessa considers her mother's drinking and crazy schemes her biggest problem. Until she meets the Genie.

When Vanessa finds a bottle on her doorstep, the last thing she expects is a wish-granting Genie. What could go wrong with a wish for her two friends and herself? Everything.

On top of that, her mothers' newest scheme is starting to unravel, and the only help Vanessa can think of is the Genie. But he's refusing to come out of his bottle. Now

Vanessa must use nothing but the truth to help her friends before her mother ruins everything.

This is a story about wishes gone wrong and a Genie who isn't telling the whole truth, served with a dash of Romance.

Buy this Short Story now and join Vanessa as she learns what it means to 'be careful what you wish for.'

https://jemmaweir.com/books/standalone/wishing-for-truths/

ABOUT AUTHOR

Too many Ideas - Never enough time

How many jobs let you build your own world? Create strange magic? Develop a diverse cast of people who will live on in the minds of others?

As an author, Jemma Weir gets to do all these things and more, as her cats chase unicorns across the breakfast table, and werewolves dig holes in the garden to torment her chihuahua, it is always an interesting day.

Fantasy books have always been her first love, from dragons to werewolves, and vampires to elves. Now, as she writes her own stories, she pulls together myths and legends, and all the crazy worlds that are her own to create stories she loves.

Working from her Scottish home, she writes fantasy, with a dash of humour, and a pinch of sass.

Want to keep up to date on new releases and get some free stories? Check out my social media or join my newsletter by clicking on the link below.

https://www.jemmaweir.com/newsletter

https://www.jemmaweir.com/blog

https://www.facebook.com/JemmaWeirAuthor

https://www.instagram.com/jemmaweir